Tori closed her eyes. "I'm scared," she whispered.

"I know. But you don't need to be. You don't ever need to be scared again." Sam moved her lips across Tori's face and Tori trembled as Sam's hands slid higher, resting just below Tori's breasts. "This is home," she said again. "And I'll be back before you know it."

Tori opened her eyes, finding Sam's. "I don't want you to go."

"And I would do anything to stay." She cupped Tori's breasts, which made Tori gasp. "I love you. And you love me. And that's all that matters."

"Yes," Tori whispered.

She pulled Sam to her, flush against her body as their mouths met. No matter how many months passed, no matter how many times they touched, how many times they made love, the intensity was still there, the want—the *need*—was still there. And her body trembled as it always did when Sam's soft hands moved across her skin.

"Make love to me," Sam murmured against her lips. "Would you please?"

Unceremoniously, Tori tossed the luggage to the floor, pulling Sam with her to the bed. She slid Sam's shirt up, exposing her small breasts. She closed her eyes for a moment, then opened them. "I love you," she whispered as her mouth found Sam's swollen nipple.

Visit

Bella Books

at

BellaBooks.com

or call our toll-free number

1-800-729-4992

In The NAME of the FATHER

GERRI HILL

Bella
BOOKS
2007

Bella Books, Inc.
P.O. Box 10543
Tallahassee, FL 32302

Printed in the United States of America on acid-free paper
First Edition

Editor: Christi Cassidy
Cover designer: LA Callaghan

ISBN-10: 1-59493-108-9
ISBN-13: 978-1-59493-108-6

About the Author

Gerri Hill has ten published works, including 2007 GCLSwinners Behind the Pine Curtainand The Killing Room, as well asGCLS finalist Hunter's Way. She began writing lesbian romanceas a way to amuse herself while snowed in one winter in themountains of Colorado, and hasn't looked back. Her first pub-lished work came in 2000 with One Summer Night. Hill's love ofnature and of being outdoors usually makes its way into her sto-ries as her characters often find themselves in beautiful naturalsettings. When she isn't writing, Hill and her longtime partner,Diane, can be found at their home in East Texas, where theirvegetable garden, orchard, and five acres of woods keep thembusy. They share their lives with Max and new puppy Casey, and an assortment of furry felines. For more, see her Web site: www.gerrihill.com.

CHAPTER ONE

"Hunter, get in here."

Tori Hunter looked up from her computer, nodding at Lieutenant Malone as she slid her chair back and walked into his office.

"Where's Kennedy?" he asked, motioning for her to sit.

Tori glanced at her watch. "She had a lunch date."

"Oh, yeah?" He cleared his throat. "Is everything okay with you two?"

Tori blushed slightly. It was still unsettling to know that her lieutenant, of all people, knew about her love life. It was one thing for Sikes to tease them, quite another to have her lieutenant asking about her relationship. "Sam was meeting her friend Amy, that's all."

"Okay. Well, you'll need to call her in. Got a situation out at Saint Mary's, downtown," he said, reading from a scribbled note

1

in his hand. "We need to be sensitive about this one, Hunter."

"Like I don't know how to be sensitive," Tori said dryly as she crossed her arms. "And if you want sensitive, maybe you should send Sikes. We've got a solid lead on our case, Lieutenant. I think we found a witness who can put Stewart at the scene. I hate to take time away from it."

"Sorry, but now you've got another case. I want you two on this one." He fingered the note again. "Father Michael was found dead this morning in the rectory. The responding unit is there, and the crime lab's already on the scene."

"A priest?" Tori asked, leaning forward. "*Homicide?*"

"Appears so. He was found naked." He looked at her. "Like I said, sensitive, Hunter. Let's try to keep the gory details from the press."

"Naked? Shouldn't this fall to the new Special Victims Unit?"

"Special Victims investigates sexual crimes, Hunter," he said, his voice tense. "This is a homicide. Nothing more."

"I understand." Tori took the piece of paper from Malone. "You're Catholic, Stan? I never knew."

He nodded. "I knew Father Michael. He was a good man."

"Okay. Sensitive."

Tori grabbed her jacket off the back of her chair. The January day was cold and rainy, making her long for summer. It had only been a couple of months since they'd gone to the boat regularly, but still, it had been an ideal summer and Tori missed it. She and Sam had spent nearly every weekend on the lake, getting to know each other without a murder investigation hanging over them. They had grown so close, Tori wondered how she had managed before Sam came into her life. But she knew, didn't she? She hadn't really been living, she had merely been existing.

She called Sam while she drove the short distance to Saint Mary's. She and Amy were still at the deli.

"Why don't you have Amy drop you off at the church?"

"Okay. We're finished anyway. I'll meet you there."

Tori had just disconnected when she was nearly sideswiped by a TV news van. She leaned on her horn, barely resisting the urge to flip them off. "Idiots."

She reached the church parking lot the same time the van did, and she held up her badge as she walked toward them. "Where the hell do you think you're going? This is a crime scene. No TV."

"Detective Hunter, we must stop meeting like this. People will start to talk."

Tori turned, silently groaning as the red-headed reporter slid from the van, long legs appearing well before the rest of her. Melissa Carter was fresh out of college, trying her best to win the evening anchor job. She had also been trying to win a date with Tori. Sam's teasing had been relentless.

"Miss Carter, please keep your crew back. We've been over this before. Crime scene, remember? It's not that hard."

"We wouldn't think of interfering with your investigation, Detective. Just trying to catch a break. Of course, I'd love an exclusive interview with you later," she purred.

Tori lifted an eyebrow. "Call my lieutenant." She walked toward the two uniformed officers standing at the steps to the church. "Make sure they stay put."

"Yes, ma'am."

Tori looked at the massive doors to the church, then back to the officers. "Where's the rectory, anyway?"

The younger of the two said, "It's the building behind the church. The M.E.'s van is there."

"Okay. What's the media look like back there?"

"Crowded. But we've got tape up." He motioned to the TV crew. "They've been run off from the back already."

"Lovely. I hate her," she murmured as she followed the sidewalk around the church. Behind it was a courtyard with several manicured gardens, assorted religious statues the centerpiece of each. It was bursting with activity as people—mostly priests and a few nuns—gathered, waiting for news.

"Detective Hunter, about time. Where's your partner?" one of the uniformed officers asked.

"She's on her way. Who's inside?"

"Crime lab and the M.E."

"Make sure the TV crews stay away. Must be a slow news day."

Tori walked inside, finding Rita Spencer bent over the body. She and the medical examiner were on better terms now. Working a serial killer case could do that.

"Spencer, anything?" Tori asked, staring at the body. He was younger than she'd assumed.

Rita looked up, nodding. "Hunter. You got this one?"

"Looks like it." Tori looked around, watching as the crime lab techs lifted prints from a fallen lamp. "What we got?"

"Strangulation. Most likely with a thin belt or a rope. See the bruising pattern?" she said, pointing to the ligature mark around the neck.

"Why do you think he's naked?"

Their eyes met.

"There is some rectal bleeding."

Tori frowned. "Raped?"

"There doesn't appear to be trauma. No visible fluids. Could be consensual. We may not know."

"*Consensual?* Jesus, he's a priest. Let's hope he was raped. I don't want to be the one to report he was having consensual sex." Then Tori paused, thinking. "Wait a minute. What about that autoerotic . . . strangulation thing? Is that the right term?"

"Asphyxiophilia. It's possible. Difficult to prove without a sexual partner, or someone who may have known he practiced it." Rita looked up. "Which was why I was expecting Special Victims, not Homicide."

Tori sighed. "Time of death?"

"Liver temp indicates he's been dead six or seven hours."

Tori looked at her watch. "It's nearly one. Do you know who found him?"

"I think the housekeeper. The responding officers took her to the kitchen."

Tori nodded. "You'll do the post, or will Jackson?"

"He'll probably want this one, Hunter."

Tori nodded again. "I understand." She walked through the house into the office where the crime lab techs were still lifting prints. "How's it look?"

"Multiple prints. In every room. I assume most belong to the priests of the diocese here." He shrugged. "And the housekeeper. I guess we could print them, then eliminate the ones that match."

"Eliminate them? Why would we want to eliminate them? We're looking for a killer."

"Hunter, they're *priests*."

"They're human. Anyone that's got a print in here, I want them accounted for. I don't care if it's the goddamn bishop." She moved next into the bedroom, eyebrows raised questioningly as the Luma Light played across the bed.

"Clean. No sign of fluids."

"Has anyone questioned the housekeeper?"

"No. She's in the kitchen."

Tori walked down the hall to the back of the house, her gaze landing on the quietly crying woman. She paused, then cleared her throat. The woman looked up, her eyes red and puffy.

"I'm Detective Hunter. I understand you found him?"

"Awful, so awful. Who would *do* this?"

"Well, we're going to find out. But I need to ask you some questions. Are you up to it?"

The woman rubbed a well-used rosary, the beads rolling between her nervous fingers. She crossed herself once, then gathered the rosary in the palm of one hand. "Yes, I'm all right. I'll help in any way. Of course I will."

Tori pulled out a chair and sat across from her, wishing Sam were here. She was better at this, more compassionate. Tori didn't usually bother with pleasantries. "What's your name?"

"Alice. I'm Alice Hagen."

Tori nodded. "Alice, what time did you find him?"

"It was nearly noon. I was running late today. I'm usually here by ten, but my husband wasn't feeling well and I was tending to him. He's got emphysema." She looked away quickly. "He was a smoker."

"How often do you come here? Daily?"

"No, no. Monday, Wednesday, Friday."

"Does anyone else—"

"Hunter? Found something," Mac, the lead technician, motioned toward the hallway.

"I'm sorry, but excuse me, Mrs. Hagen. I'll be right back."

Tori followed him back into the living room, then outside. She looked up once into the gray sky, then brushed at the moisture that had gathered on her hair.

"Found these in the shrubs," he said, pointing to what looked like men's pajamas. "And a belt." He motioned for her to follow. "Got shoe prints. Going to take a cast of them. There're only two. This one is smeared, like he was running."

"Great. Maybe we can get a print off the belt," she said, watching as the belt was carefully placed in an evidence bag. "Or fluids on the clothes." She nodded at the officer who found them. "Good job. Make sure Spencer gets the belt. See if it matches her ligature mark."

Sam hurried through the fine drizzle, excusing herself as she moved among the crowd that had gathered. She spotted Tori at the edge of the house and slowed, an involuntary smile touching her lips before she could stop it. Tori was so . . . so powerful, so totally in control, and Sam was as drawn to her today as she'd been last year when she'd first transferred to Homicide. Slowly shaking her head, she marveled at all the changes in her life since then. The biggest change, having fallen in love with a woman. For the first time, she was totally happy with her life, both professionally and personally. And she was continually amazed that she and Tori could leave the job at the end of the day and have a completely different life at home, one that involved getting to know each other away from work, away from the stress of a murder investigation. And as she'd suspected, Tori had a wicked sense of humor. It was a part of her personality that she'd kept hidden as she'd retreated from life. But little by little, she'd opened up, and now she was practically best buddies with John Sikes, something Sam never thought could be possible.

As she stared, she saw Tori's back straighten and her head tilt to the side. Then, like always, she turned, Tori's eyes capturing her own in an instant. With only a slight twitch of her lips and one raised eyebrow, she turned back to Mac.

How does she do that?

Sam hurried on, the light mist turning into a downright drizzle. Inside the rectory, she sidestepped Rita Spencer who was preparing to bring the body out.

"Rita," she said by way of greeting.

Rita nodded. "The housekeeper is still in the kitchen. I don't think Hunter had a chance to question her."

"Thanks."

Sam turned, watching the activity in the bedroom before moving down the hallway and into the kitchen. She paused, offering a slight smile as the older woman turned tear-stained cheeks her way.

"I'm Detective Kennedy. I'm sorry, but I don't know your name."

"Alice Hagen. Isn't it just so awful, Detective?"

"Yes, ma'am, it is." Sam pulled out one of the chairs by the kitchen table and sat down. "Are you the one who found him,

7

Alice?"

"I came in here, through the kitchen, like always. But it was too quiet. I knew something was wrong."

"Tell me what you saw."

"Well, I called to him but got no answer. At first, I thought that maybe he'd gone on to the church, but he always worked in his office, going over his sermon until I brought him his lunch."

"You came every day?"

"No, like I was telling that other policewoman, I come three days a week. The other two days, he fends for himself." Then she smiled. "Or one of the ladies from the church will drop off a meal." She leaned forward. "He was so well-liked. No one wanted him to do without," she said quietly.

Sam nodded. "So, you called out to him. Then what?"

"Well, I went to his office first. But before I could open the door, I saw . . . oh dear God, I saw him lying there, *naked*."

"Where was he when you found him, Alice?"

"In the den, he was just . . . *lying* there," she finished in a whisper.

Sam nodded again, reaching out to touch the older woman's arm. "Tell me what's out of order. The den area looks disturbed, as if there was a struggle."

"Oh, yes. I always kept it so neat. It's a mess. Just awful."

"Yes, I understand. Did you touch anything? Did you touch him?"

"Oh, no. I didn't touch anything. Well, the phone, you know. When I called," she said.

Sam jotted down some notes, then glanced up when she heard footsteps approach.

Tori looked at her briefly, then turned her attention to Alice Hagen. "Mrs. Hagen, excuse me, but . . . I have a few more questions if you're up for it."

"Of course, Officer."

"And forgive me for the bluntness of this, but were you aware

8

of Father Michael having any . . . well, any sexual partners?"

The gasp sounded nearly like a groan. "*Sexual*? He was a *priest*! Of course he didn't have any . . . *partners*." She brought the tissue to her eyes again as she cried. "What kind of police are you?"

Tori ran a hand through her hair which was glistening with raindrops. "Of course. I'm sorry." Then she looked again at Sam. "All done?"

Sam stood up. "Yes. Thank you, Mrs. Hagen. You've been a big help." She handed the older woman her card. "If you think of anything else, anything at all, please call me." She followed Tori out into the hallway, stopping her with a light touch on the arm. "Sexual partners?" she murmured.

"Either that or he was raped. We'll know more after the post."

"*Raped?*" Sam looked down the hall back to where Mrs. Hagen still sat. "Okay. Do we want to look for witnesses? There were a lot of people in the courtyard. Other priests, nuns. Maybe someone saw something out of the ordinary."

"Father Michael obviously lived alone. Where does everyone else stay?"

"I'm not sure. But the diocese headquarters is located here, and the seminary. And there's a small convent just two blocks away. Word has spread, I'm sure." Sam pointed down the hall as a priest stood talking to one of the uniformed officers. "This looks like an official visit."

Tori followed her gaze, and Sam noticed the older priest look their way. He was an overweight man, his face round and puffy. He took off his black hat as he made his way over to them. Bushy, graying hair protruded like two patches above his ears; the rest of his head was as slick as a cue ball.

"Excuse me. I'm Monsignor Bernard. Bishop Lewis sent me," he said, his hand extended to both her and Tori. "The officers over there said that you were going to be investigating this tragedy. Is that correct?"

Before Sam could speak, Tori stepped forward.

"I'm Detective Hunter, and this is Detective Kennedy. What can we do for you?"

"As I said, Bishop Lewis sent me to oversee this situation. For the time being."

Tori raised an eyebrow. "Oversee?"

"With the press, mainly. We are aware of how the situation looks, Detective. And by no means can the Dallas Diocese handle another scandal."

"Monsignor, if you have information about Father Michael's private life, you need to tell us now."

"If you're insinuating that Father Michael behaved inappropriately, Detective, you are very wrong. Father Michael has an impeccable record and there has never been even a hint of improper behavior."

"Then what scandal are you trying to avoid?" Sam asked.

"When the press reports that a priest was found naked and that there was evidence of sexual activity, do you think the words *raped* or *assaulted* will be included in the text? No. They will assume sexual misconduct. And we simply can't have that."

"Monsignor, how do you know what evidence was found? There have been no official statements."

He smiled but shook his head. "I won't bore you with the chain of information, Detectives. What we want, in your official statement to the press, is for you to report that he was sexually assaulted and not leave it up to the reporters to use their own words."

Tori said, "I'm sorry. I can't do that. I don't know if he was sexually assaulted or not. I won't know until the medical examiner issues his report." Her cell rang and she unclipped it from her belt. "Excuse me," she murmured as she moved back into the kitchen.

❧

"Hunter, I just got a call from CIU."

Tori rolled her eyes. CIU—Criminal Investigative Unit—thought they were the damn FBI. "And?"

"We're not to talk to the press on this one. They're going to handle it. I think they're sending someone over now."

Tori sighed. "Great, Lieutenant. Are they going to handle the goddammed investigation, too?"

"Look, I told you this was sensitive. Apparently, the bishop contacted the mayor and the mayor himself called the chief. The church is concerned about—"

"They're concerned about a sex scandal. They don't appear too concerned about their dead priest, only how it's going to look in the papers."

"Well, as much as you hate dealing with the press, I thought you'd love this." Malone paused. "Now did you find anything at the scene?"

"They found pajamas and a belt under some shrubs. The belt could likely be the murder weapon. Multiple prints in the house. We got nothing at this point, really."

"Well, we need to find something."

"No shit," Tori murmured after she'd disconnected. Sam and the monsignor were still talking in the hallway, his bulk nearly dwarfing Sam. Tori said to him, "Well, your prayers have been answered, it seems. They're sending someone over to handle the press."

"Thank you, Detective."

"I assure you, I had nothing to do with it. Now, if you'll excuse us," she said, brushing past him and motioning for Sam to follow.

"Who's coming over?" Sam asked when they stepped outside. "CIU."

"CIU? Are they taking over the case?"

"I wish." Tori stopped and looked to the sky, wondering how long before the downpour hit. "Let's find out if anyone saw anything this morning."

"Starting where?"

"I don't know. Grab a nun."

Sam smiled. "Grab a nun?"

Their eyes met and Tori allowed herself a brief smile. "Maybe I should take the nuns. You have more of a history with priests."

"My brother doesn't count. But maybe you're right. I think you're less likely to piss off the nuns."

"Funny, Detective," Tori said as she moved away, finding a group of four nuns watching them.

CHAPTER TWO

"Hunter, I hear you got close to a church today and lightning didn't strike!" John Sikes said with a laugh.

"Good one, Sikes. I can always count on you for humor in the midst of death," Tori said as she picked up her coffee cup. Eyeing the dark liquid—which she assumed was several hours old—she opted for a water bottle instead, grabbing one from the small fridge tucked in the corner.

"Heard about the priest, but what about your homeless guy?"

"Finally got a witness who picked out Stewart's picture. But—"

"But it's another homeless guy?"

"Exactly. A defense attorney would have him for lunch." Tori pulled her chair out with her foot before sitting down. "Saturday night was fun. Thanks for asking us."

"Oh, sure. We usually get together at least once a month to play. Sorry you two had to come separately."

Tori shrugged. "Better to be safe."

"I had no idea Sam could play poker."

"I'd been teaching her all last week. She picked it up pretty quickly."

"She looked like she had a great time." He leaned on the corner of her desk. "And Ronnie's an asshole," John said quietly. "Sorry about that."

"Sam can handle herself. No big deal."

"Yeah, but it was you I was worried about. You should have seen the look on your face when he tried to kiss her."

Tori smiled. "He doesn't know how close he was to having a gun shoved up his ass."

John laughed and stood, slipping his hands into his pockets. "So, what's with the priest?"

"Don't know yet. He was found naked, strangled. Spencer found rectal bleeding, but we don't know if it was assault or consensual. Jackson was going to do the post."

"Oh, man. You better hope the M.E. states it as assault. It'll be a regular circus otherwise."

"It's already a circus. CIU's pulled rank. They're handling the media. I guess they're afraid I might say something off-color."

"Now where would they get that idea? But shouldn't Special Victims take this one? I mean, isn't that why they formed that unit? To take this kind of crap off our hands?"

Sam watched from across the squad room, smiling as Tori and John laughed together. Last year, the two could hardly tolerate each other's presence. Now, they were buddies. And Tori needed a buddy. She needed someone other than Sam in her life, someone else to let her know that she was a good person, worthy of friendship. Oh, she could still be a total bitch, especially when things didn't go the way she wanted. But finally, she was dropping the shield around her and letting everyone else see the

14

person who Sam had fallen in love with. And John Sikes was not immune to Tori's charms, Sam knew. John had joined them often on the boat at Eagle Mountain Lake, his love of fishing nearly matching that of Tori's.

Tori must have felt her presence, turning to look at her, her face gentling. Here in their own squad room, they didn't have to be so careful. It was unspoken, but everyone knew about their relationship. Even Gary Walker, Donaldson's new partner, acknowledged it. It went without saying that it remain in-house. As far as the other detectives were concerned, if Lieutenant Malone didn't have a problem with it, they didn't have a problem with it.

"Trying to sneak up on us?"

"And someday I just might." She squeezed John's arm as she passed. "Hey, Sikes. Where were you this morning?"

"Ramirez wanted to check out a hunch. We spent half the night and all this morning staking out a neighborhood bar in Oak Cliff."

Sam wrinkled her nose. She hated stakeouts. "Sorry. Any luck?"

"Of course not." He shoved off the corner of Tori's desk. "Catch you two later."

Sam leaned across her desk, watching Tori. "Any luck with your nuns?"

"No. What about you? Enjoy your ride over in the patrol car?"

"No. He wouldn't let me play with anything." Sam picked up the file, knowing Tori had already typed up her notes. She glanced through them quickly, seeing the few comments Tori had added after speaking to the nuns. "Father Michael was very popular."

"Apparently so."

Sam leaned her elbows on her desk, watching Tori. "Who in their right mind would kill a priest?"

Tori leaned back, twisting a pen between her fingers. "People kill for revenge. People kill out of anger. People kill for spite. People kill for fun." She raised her eyebrows. "You kill a priest, which of those would be a good reason?"

"Revenge." Sam shrugged, thinking for a moment. "Or anger."

"Why would you be angry at a priest?"

Sam's eyes widened. "I would be angry at a priest if he molested me."

Tori nodded. "So, our killer could be a former altar boy, perhaps, taking out his anger now? Or maybe exacting revenge?"

"But Monsignor Bernard said that Father Michael had no complaints, not even a hint of inappropriate behavior," Sam reminded her.

"Just because he said it doesn't mean it's true."

Sam bit her lower lip, then smiled. She was raised Catholic, and her brother was a priest, so it never occurred to her that the monsignor could be lying. "That just wouldn't be right."

"Sam, just because he's a priest, don't assume anything. Don't assume they're not withholding something from us. Don't assume Father Michael didn't have consensual sex. And don't assume, because they're priests, that they're not human."

Sam agreed. "You're right. I have this skewed opinion, I know."

"And I'm too cynical about it all," Tori admitted. "So we need to find a common ground. Maybe we should—"

"Hunter? Crime lab's on line two," Fisk bellowed from the front desk.

"That was quick," she said before punching the speakerphone button. "Hunter. What do you have?"

"We got a good print off the belt, Hunter. It matched a partial that was found on the lamp."

"Got a name?"

"Juan Hidalgo. He's been in and out. Assault, armed robbery, possession."

"Can you e-mail me the specifics?"

"Already done."

"Thanks." She looked at Sam. "Juan Hidalgo? I think one of the nuns mentioned his name."

Sam looked at her notes, flipping through the pages. "Here he is. Handyman. He works three or four days a week."

Tori opened her e-mail, scanning it briefly before printing it. "Got an address. Little Mexico."

"Of course it'd be Little Mexico." Sam looked around, hoping Tony was at his desk. They'd found from experience that it helped to have a Spanish-speaking officer with them. But Ramirez and Sikes had disappeared.

"Let's tell Malone," Tori said, hurrying into the lieutenant's office.

Sam waited at the stairs, keys dangling from her fingers.

Tori grinned when she saw them. "Got the Lexus?"

"Only the best for you, Hunter," Sam said in a sultry voice.

They paused at the door, gazing at each other, a smile playing across Tori's face. Tori's gaze dropped to Sam's lips for only a second, but it was enough. Sam took a breath, saw Tori's eyes darken.

"How can you do that to me with just a look?" Sam whispered.

Tori only smiled, lightly touching Sam's back as they went down the stairs.

Tori drove as Sam looked at the e-mail again, then their street finder on the laptop. "It's a housing project. Should be the next block."

"Damn, but this is run-down," Tori muttered, wondering if Juan Hidalgo lived with his family or alone. "It looks worse than my building."

"Oh, I'd say they're about the same, sweetheart."

Tori laughed. "Three hundred dollars a month rent. You can't beat it."

"Especially when you don't actually *live* there."

"You're ready for me to give it up?"

"Tori, you've not set foot in the apartment since May."

"Has it been that long?"

Sam reached over and squeezed Tori's thigh. "Keep it as long as you want."

Tori parked along the curb and cut the engine. "I don't really feel the need to keep it anymore. It's just, well, I haven't had time to think about moving my stuff out. Besides, what would I do with it all?"

"Just stop paying rent. They'll give your furniture away to someone who needs it."

Tori looked up at the three-story building, then went with Sam toward the front doors. One of the doors was propped open, letting in the chill from the cold January day. "I think I've got a bottle of Scotch," Tori murmured.

"What?"

"At my apartment. And some old files and stuff."

Not waiting for a response, which she didn't expect anyway, Tori headed on up the stairs. Files. Files of her family's murder. She realized she hadn't mentioned her family since the night she'd told Sam about their murder, but she'd kept copies of all the old case files.

"Then why don't you bring them to our place?" Sam said.

Tori paused in mid-step. *Our place.* How she loved those words. After Internal Affairs finished their investigation last year, Sam gave up her apartment and the two of them moved into an older complex hidden away near White Rock Lake. It was a small lake compared to the expanse of Eagle Mountain, where they kept their boat. But here, they were only two blocks from the city lake, and Tori often went there in the evenings to fish and to satisfy her need for solitude. Sam understood she needed her quiet time—her

18

alone time—and she never questioned it. And Tori knew it also gave Sam some time alone to catch up with friends, mainly Amy.

But get rid of her old apartment? Well, she *was* throwing away three hundred bucks a month just to keep it. "Okay," she finally said, glancing back at Sam.

Sam frowned. "Okay what?"

"Maybe this weekend we could go to my apartment and pack up a few things."

Smiling, Sam seemed surprised. "Oh. Okay. Sure."

Tori stopped at the second-floor landing, looking up into the dark stairwell. "He would have to be on the third floor, wouldn't he?"

"Does it smell in here to you?"

"Yeah. I told you it was worse than my building."

Before Sam could reply, running footsteps below made them both stop and look back. Two uniformed police officers were running up the stairs.

"Stand back, ladies!" one of them shouted as they ran past them.

Tori and Sam pressed against the wall, out of their way, Tori glaring at their retreating backs. "Idiots," she muttered.

"What are the chances they're going to the same apartment we are?"

"With our luck, they'll chase our guy off." Tori started toward the third floor, quickening her pace. "Come on."

They were both out of breath as they raced up the steps, looking in the direction of the commotion down the hallway. Loud voices, all in Spanish, called out, trying to talk over the others.

"What room are we?" Tori asking, gasping.

"Three twelve."

"Well, this is just fucking great," Tori muttered as she caught her breath. "*They're* in room three twelve."

Tori stood in the doorway, noting the chaos inside, watching as the two officers tried in vain to usher the crowd away from a body on the floor.

One of the officers looked up and saw her, motioning for her to stop. "You cannot come in here, ma'am. You need to go back into the hallway. This is a crime scene."

"And I see you're doing a wonderful job of securing it." She held up her badge. "Detectives Hunter and Kennedy. Homicide."

"Damn, that was quick. Usually takes you guys an hour to show up."

Tori looked around. "Who are all these people and why the *hell* are they contaminating this crime scene?"

The voices grew louder, the quickly spoken Spanish bouncing around Tori.

She finally threw her arms up, yelling. "Shut up! Everyone shut up!" When the room was quiet, except for the wailing sobs of an older woman, she continued, "Can anyone here speak English? *Por favor?* English?"

Silence ensued as their gazes followed her around the room.

She tried again. "English? Anyone?"

One man finally stepped forward. "*Si. Un poco.*"

Tori gritted her teeth, wondering why in the hell she'd never learned to speak Spanish. "*Como te llamas?*"

The man nodded. "Hector Ybarra."

Tori pointed at the man on the floor. "Who is he?"

"Juan. Juan Hidalgo."

At the man's words, the older woman started wailing again. Tori and Sam locked eyes, Sam nodding as she moved into the hallway, already dialing her cell.

"The mother?" Tori asked Hector.

"*Si, es la mama.*"

"Okay. Ask everyone to leave this apartment, please."

The man frowned.

Tori rubbed her head, trying to control her temper. "Leave. Go. Out," she said, shooing them toward the door.

"*Si.*"

Tori grabbed his arm. "Not you." She watched as the others were led from the room, the two officers having to forcibly remove the crying woman. "Nine-one-one?"

"I call."

She made her hand into a gun and pointed it at Juan. "You see?"

"No, no." He pointed to his ear. "*Oye.*"

She motioned out the door. "Did *mama* see? Did she live with him?"

"No, no. Next door."

"Okay. *Gracias.*" She motioned to the door. "Go." She turned, staring at the body of their only suspect. "Well, this sucks the big one."

"How bad is it?" Sam asked from behind her.

"It's totally contaminated. They moved the body, for one thing. Looks like they flipped him over. Someone got blood on their shoes," she said, pointing to the prints.

"Window is open. Cold day like today, I doubt he had it open for air. Especially now. It's nearly dark outside."

Tori circled the body, careful not to touch anything. "Fire escape right outside."

"Is it down?"

Tori went to the window and sighed. "Yep." She looked back to the door. "But no forced entry. Could have known the shooter."

There was a rustling in the hallway, then Mac stuck his head inside. "Ladies, we meet again."

"Sorry, Mac, but there were probably ten people in this room when we got here," Sam said. "Don't know if you're going to find much."

"We'll sift through it." He looked at their body. "Damn, who walked in my blood pool?"

Sam shrugged. "They also don't speak English." Sam stepped

21

aside as Rita Spencer walked in, medical bag on one shoulder, camera on the other.

"Well, this has got to be a first," Rita said, "you two beating me to a scene."

"Yeah, well, we came here hoping to find him alive, not dead," Tori said. "And why did they send you again?"

"Jackson's started the post on your priest." Rita bent down, then shook her head. "He's been moved." She looked up sharply. "Who the hell moved my body?"

"I would guess his mother," Tori said. "Or any of the other nine people who were in here."

"Why do you guys have this one, anyway? The priest not enough for you?"

"Meet Juan Hidalgo. Our only suspect in Father Michael's murder."

"Damn, Hunter. What are the chances of that?"

"I would have guessed none." She turned to Sam, who was busy talking on her cell again. Her animated expression told Tori she was describing the scene.

She looked up, meeting Tori's eyes as she disconnected. "Lieutenant says he wants Ramirez and Sikes on this one, not us."

"Why not us?"

Sam folded her phone and slipped it into her jacket pocket. "Well, the Spanish, for one thing. And we already have two open cases."

Tori pointed at Juan Hidalgo. "This case and the priest are linked. This is not a fucking coincidence," she snapped.

Sam shrugged. "Feel free to call him. I'm just passing on his orders."

Tori shook her head. "Sorry," she said quietly, her eyes darting from Sam to Rita. *Orders.* "Okay, Spencer. We're out of here. The guys will be in touch."

"Can't wait," Rita murmured absently, her camera already going to work.

CHAPTER THREE

"Shower first or dinner?"

"Shower," Tori said, already pulling her sweater over her head.

"Share?" Sam asked quietly, her voice low—inviting.

Tori stopped and turned, meeting Sam's gentle gaze. The smoldering desire she saw there never failed to amaze her. She nodded. "Yeah. Share."

She tossed her sweater on the bed and kicked off her shoes, watching as Sam did the same. Her breath caught as Sam pulled her undershirt off. There was no bra to distract her. Going slowly to Sam, she pulled her own black sports bra off and tossed it on the floor without looking.

"You're so beautiful, Sam," Tori whispered, reaching out to cup Sam's small breasts.

Sam moved into Tori's touch, pulling Tori close as her mouth found Tori's. "Shower," she murmured.

Tori knew it was one of her most favorite things—showering together. There would be no words, only the quiet touching, stroking, as they stood under the warm water. Sam lowered the zipper on Tori's jeans with practiced ease. Her hands slipped around Tori's hips, squeezing the firm buttocks, until Tori moaned.

"I swear, I'll never tire of this."

Tori smiled against her lips, then pulled away. "Come on. Shower," she reminded her. She led Sam into the bathroom, releasing her long enough for them both to shed their remaining clothes.

CHAPTER FOUR

"Wait a minute. A consultant? What the hell for?"

Malone sighed. "In case you don't already know this, the chief doesn't have to offer an explanation, Hunter. I only know she flew in from Boston last night and she's from some hotshot public relations firm."

Tori paced in front of his desk while Sam looked on silently. Tori finally stopped, the frustration evident on her face as she rested her hands on her hips. "How the hell are we supposed to do our job with a goddammed public relations consultant following us around? Talk about a circus, well this is it."

"She won't be following you around. She'll be dealing with the media, mainly. She'll issue formal statements for the diocese and deal with questions. And if we have questions for the diocese, we'll go through her. But she won't have any bearing on our investigation, Hunter." He stared at her. "Now sit down, please."

"How long will we be able to sit on the M.E.'s report?" Sam asked. "The press is going to want some information."

"Well, that's the beauty of this, Kennedy. We don't have to sit on anything. All media reports will come directly from the chief's office."

Tori stared at him. "I didn't realize the Catholic Church wielded that much power over us, Lieutenant."

"I believe Bishop Lewis and the mayor are quite close, Hunter. Not that it's our concern."

She shrugged. "That's fine. I just hate when politics play a part in one of our investigations."

They all turned at the light knocking on the door.

Malone motioned for Sikes and Ramirez to come in and said, "We're going to have a group effort on this case, Hunter. Obviously we can't look at Juan Hidalgo's death as a coincidence, so we'll assume it's linked to Father Michael. Tony, I want you and John on that one." He paused. "Hunter, you and Kennedy get the priest. I know you've already done some interviews, but we'll need to go deeper. Find out his routine, find out who visited the rectory the most."

"Saint Mary's is a large church with several priests," Sam said. "Any idea how Father Michael came to live at the rectory and none of the others did? I wouldn't think seniority, considering how young he was."

Malone shook his head. "I'm not what you'd call a regular churchgoer. I knew Father Michael from the handful of times I went there. But I have no idea about their living arrangements."

"It looked like it was several bedrooms. Maybe he wasn't the only one who lived there. Could have had roommates," Sam suggested.

But Tori shook her head. "We both talked to the housekeeper. She never once gave any indication that someone else lived there. The other two bedrooms were too impersonal.

Nothing more than guest rooms."

"From your notes, Hunter, Juan Hidalgo worked there for several years," Sikes said. "But why would they keep him on? He's been in and out of jail for the last seven years. Did time for armed robbery. Was in most recently in June of last year for possession of marijuana."

"They're a church. I would assume they're in the business of reforming and rehabilitating," Tori said. "Why else?"

"Maybe they didn't know," Tony said. "I mean, if he's a parishioner and needed work, I doubt they'd do a background check."

"And his was the only print on the belt?" Malone asked.

"His and Father Michael's."

Tori stood and started pacing the room. "So Hidalgo walks in on Father Michael and someone having sex. He freaks out. Trashes the room. Scares off the other guy." She stopped pacing. "Or woman. We're just assuming here." She turned, her arms outstretched. "Takes the belt, strangles the priest. Then panics. Grabs his pajamas and the belt, and runs."

"If he's going to go to the trouble of grabbing the belt, why drop it in the shrubs where anyone is bound to find it?" Sam asked.

"And I don't want to assume a sexual partner, Hunter," Malone said. "Lab report is not back and Jackson has not given us the results of the post," he reminded her.

"I saw the body. I talked to Spencer. There was evidence of sexual activity and it did not appear to be forced."

"Well, we're trying to find out who killed him, not whether he was having sex or not," Malone said sharply. "Keep that in mind."

"Well, unless the post tells us something we're not expecting, then all we have is circumstantial evidence linking Hidalgo. A print on the overturned lamp and a print on the belt. There has to be a motive. And there was nothing of value missing, so not robbery."

"What if Father Michael found out about Hidalgo, found out he'd been in jail? Hidalgo could have been afraid he would lose his job. Could be motive," Sikes said.

"But Hidalgo took a bullet to the head at point-blank range," Sam reminded them. "So if we're considering the two murders are linked, whoever killed Juan Hidalgo knew about Father Michael."

"Knew what?" Tori asked. "Knew he was killed? Knew he was having sex? What?"

"So maybe Hidalgo's death is revenge for killing Father Michael," Sikes suggested.

Tori nodded. "Which means there's a third party."

"Okay, back to the beginning," Malone said. "Father Michael was killed between five and six a.m., based on Spencer's preliminary findings. We're at the scene before one yesterday afternoon. By three, we're notified of the print on the belt. And before four o'clock, Hidalgo is shot and killed. Ten hours."

Sam leaned forward, tapping lightly on Malone's desk. "It seems obvious, doesn't it?"

He looked at her. "What?"

"Whoever was with Father Michael, whoever Hidalgo walked in on, he—or she—would know Hidalgo was the one who killed the priest. He hears on the news that Father Michael has been killed. He knows who walked in on them. So, to protect himself and to protect Father Michael's name, he kills Hidalgo."

Malone shrugged. "It's a theory, Kennedy. Thin at best."

Tori nodded. "And we're all basing this on the assumption Hidalgo is our killer. What if he found Father Michael dead, he touches him, then gets scared. Maybe he took the belt and pajamas, maybe they were just lying beside the body. Maybe he took them to protect the priest. But once outside, the real killer is still there. So Juan tosses the belt and pajamas and takes off running. His print is on the belt. His boot print is on the ground. But he's not the killer." She shrugged. "Circumstantial evidence."

"There's just one thing," Ramirez said. "Why was Juan Hidalgo at the rectory at five in the morning?"

"And I think we're overlooking one other scenario," Sikes said. "No one has mentioned the possibility of Hidalgo being the sexual partner. Maybe that's why he was there at five."

"Oh, come on, man. Hidalgo was a lowlife," Ramirez said. "No way."

"Why not?" Sikes shot back. "They have sex. Hidalgo freaks out for whatever reason, then kills Father Michael. Takes the belt and pajamas, thinking it may have DNA."

Tori laughed. "John, do you really think Hidalgo was meticulous enough to even consider DNA evidence left behind?"

"I have to agree," Sam said. "We saw Hidalgo. We saw where he lived. He didn't have a TV. His family didn't speak English. I seriously doubt he knows the procedures of a crime lab and how evidence is obtained." Sam shrugged. "Besides, he didn't take the evidence with him, or hide it. It was carelessly tossed in the bushes, as if he wanted it to be found."

"Which brings us back to the possibility that he was startled by someone. Startled, so he dumped the clothes and belt, and then took off."

"Which again leaves us with a third party," Sikes said.

Tori sighed. "And still no closer to a motive or a suspect."

CHAPTER FIVE

Sam tossed her purse on her desk and strode purposely toward the coffee. "Tori wouldn't let me stop for *real* coffee." She stared at the pot. "How bad is it this morning?" she asked John.

"Define *bad*."

Sam crinkled up her nose as she poured, wondering why she didn't just switch to herbal tea or something.

"Where's Tori?"

"She walked over to the lab. Jackson said he had the report ready."

John looked past Sam, motioning across the squad room as an impeccably dressed woman walked through. "Nice."

"Our consultant?" Sam whispered.

"Kinda ironic, isn't it?"

"What do you mean?"

"Well, you know, the Catholic Church's stance on homosexuality isn't real friendly to your kind. I'm surprised they have a lesbian working for them."

Sam turned and frowned. "A lesbian?" She looked back at the attractive young woman who stood talking to Malone. Her black business suit hugged her slim hips, dark blond hair, long and straight, tucked behind her ears, her makeup applied to perfection. A diamond on her ring flashed as she talked and Sam shook her head. "She's not gay, John."

John laughed. "I swear, your gaydar still doesn't work, does it?" He leaned closer, his voice low. "Didn't you see her walk? She's got that cocky walk like Hunter has. And I bet you ten bucks her handshake will crack your fingers."

"I'm sure Tori will appreciate you saying her walk is cocky. I happen to think it's sexy as hell."

He nudged her. "So? Ten bucks?"

"You're on. Because no way she's gay."

John cleared his throat. "We're about to find out."

Malone, a smile on his face, ushered the attractive woman over. Sam doubted he'd be smiling if Tori were here, knowing Tori's feeling about the consultant.

"Kennedy, Sikes, I want you to meet Marissa Goodard. She's the consultant I told you about."

"Actually, it's Goddard, Lieutenant." The woman smiled at Sam. "Kennedy or Sikes?"

Sam glanced at the lieutenant, noticing his slightly flushed face. She knew he wasn't used to being dismissed so easily. "Samantha Kennedy."

"Nice to meet you, Samantha."

Sam took her hand, nearly cringing as the strong fingers gripped her own and squeezed tightly. She watched as the woman reached for John's hand.

"John Sikes. A pleasure, Ms. Goddard." His smile was pronounced as he looked at Sam. "Ten bucks," he mouthed at her.

"Where's Hunter?"

"She's at the lab, Lieutenant."

"They got reports for us?"

"Spencer did the post on Hidalgo. Everything's back but toxicology. Jackson was going to meet with her," Sam explained.

"Find out when she'll be back. I want us to meet with Ms. Goddard here. She'll have some questions before she meets with the press this afternoon."

"I understand the mayor has set up a press conference for this afternoon," Ms. Goddard said. "Who will be issuing a statement on behalf of the police department?"

"The mayor's office is handling that as well."

She smiled. "I see. Well, I understand it's a delicate situation. We wouldn't want one of your officers to say something out of line."

"We're well aware that it's delicate, Ms. Goddard," Sam said with just a hint of irritation. "It's also highly unusual for the mayor's office to oversee a murder investigation."

"Believe me, Samantha, you don't want to be on the receiving end of reporters' questions regarding a murdered priest. It's a potential scandal waiting to break and they can be ruthless." She smiled again. "And please call me Marissa."

"Of course."

"And this Hunter person," she said, tapping impatiently at her gold wristwatch. "I have appointments set up. I don't have time for a delay." She looked pointedly at Sam. "We're not going to have a problem with punctuality with her, are we?"

Sam opened her mouth to speak, and then closed it. She glanced at Malone before forcing a smile to her face. "Let me call her." She grasped John's arm and led him toward the door. "Oh, this is going to be fun," she whispered.

Tori sat patiently as she watched Jackson unwrap a piece of gum and methodically fold it into thirds before placing it into his mouth. It was a habit that both irritated her and fascinated her. But she'd learned that Jackson was never ready to proceed until after the gum ritual.

Now, he put his reading glasses on and opened the file, his brows drawn together.

Tori finally leaned forward and said, "You're testing my good mood, Jackson. What do you have?"

"Sorry, Hunter. I hadn't had a chance to read Spencer's report on Mr. Hidalgo." He looked up. "Not much, actually. Single GSW to the right temporal lobe. Thirty-eight caliber. Full tox reports aren't back yet, but his blood alcohol content was point oh-nine."

"Damn. Drunk on his ass," she said.

Jackson nodded and handed her a file. "Here's Mac's initial report. I understand the scene was contaminated."

"Yeah. We were there." Tori flipped through it, scanning the words, noting nothing unusual. She closed it and looked up. "The priest?"

He shook his head. "Not much on him either. Cause of death was strangulation. No unusual bruising other than around the neck. Rectal bleeding appears to be from recent intercourse. No fluids. There was no trauma to indicate assault. But that doesn't necessarily mean there wasn't. It just means there was no bruising. Toxicology will be back on him this afternoon, but prelim blood work was clean." He leaned back. "The belt found in the bushes matches the ligature marks on the neck."

"Thanks, Jackson. Do you mind e-mailing Sikes your final report on Hidalgo?"

"No problem."

"What about Mac's report on the priest? Do you have it yet?"

He shook his head. "He was still working on it. They had a lot more to process there."

"Okay. I'll go bug him. Thanks."

Tori was at the door when he called to her.

"Hunter, what's this I hear about a public relations firm?"

"We don't know much more. Mayor's office agreed to it. Some hotshot firm from Boston. Malone said they handled the abuse scandal the Church had up there several years ago."

"It's highly unusual to try to handle the press this way. It may end up pissing them off and cause them to dig deeper, not go away."

"This case has scandal written all over it. Yeah, the press will be hard to fend off, consultant or not."

He folded his case file neatly, then tossed it on the corner of his desk. "Well, perhaps Mac found something useful for you."

But Tori found he hadn't. Not really.

"No fluids," Mac said when she caught up with him at the crime lab. "But we've got epithelia from two sources in the master bedroom."

Tori raised her eyebrows. Tissue samples would help, but still circumstantial. "Bed?"

"On the sheets." He nodded. "One is a match for your dead priest. The other is unknown."

Tori stared at him.

"Unknown male," Mac clarified. He flipped through the file. "Got thirteen usable prints from the rectory. We ran them all. Only Hidalgo's came back with a hit."

"We're going to try to get the names of people who would have had cause to be in there. Like the housekeeper, obviously. Normally we'd just get a warrant and print everyone so we could match them up. But with the mayor's office involved, with CIU nosing around and now a goddammed consultant for the church, I'd say a warrant is going to be hard to come by."

"Consultant?"

"Yeah. If I need to talk to someone at the church, I have to go through this consultant first. And if I get asked a question by the lovely—but irritating—Melissa Carter from Channel Five, I get to blow her off and tell her to hound the consultant instead."

Mac laughed. "Yeah, she's a looker but I hear she's a pain in the ass."

"That she is." Tori let out a heavy sigh. "Okay, Mac, what else you got?"

"Shoe prints were a size eleven. They were a match for a pair we found in Hidalgo's apartment." He shrugged. "Cause of death, strangulation. Murder weapon was the belt. Belt had Hidalgo's prints on it." He shrugged again. "Like I said, not much. Maybe matching the shoe print will be enough."

"He worked there. Wouldn't be unusual for his shoe prints to be outside. Right?" She flipped through the Hidalgo file again. "And nothing at the scene? What about the fire escape?"

"We got smudges, that's all. Could be from anyone though. Having that window opened could have just been a decoy. There was no evidence of a forced entry. We can assume the killer entered and left the same way."

"Would the killer have had time to shoot and run before anyone saw him? Judging from all the people in the room, they came running as soon as they heard the shot."

"Look at it this way," Mac said. "You shoot. Do you have time to open the window, get out, drop the ladder and head down before someone in the room sees you?"

Tori nodded slowly. "You're right. The fastest exit would have been the door. But if that's the case, he wouldn't have had time to open the window regardless."

"So maybe the window was open all along. Maybe Hidalgo always opened it."

Tori took a deep breath and let it out slowly. "So I've got a dead priest who we think Juan Hidalgo killed. And now we've got a dead Juan Hidalgo with absolutely no evidence as to who killed him." She looked at Mac. "Any suggestions?"

Mac shook his head. "Sorry, Hunter. But we did get four usable prints from inside the apartment that weren't Hidalgo's. No hits on them. And none of them match the unknown prints from the rectory."

"Well, I'll have Sikes and Ramirez try to track down those four prints." She stood. "Thanks, Mac."

"We'll have full tox reports tomorrow. Something might turn up there."

"Yeah. Let me know."

CHAPTER SIX

"Where have you been?" Sam hissed when Tori strolled nonchalantly into the squad room at eleven. She glanced quickly toward Malone's office. "She's like a piranha."

"Like I told you on the phone, she can kiss my ass. I don't work for her." Tori pulled out her chair with her foot, then tossed Sam the files. "Mac made copies for me. He'll e-mail the final report, probably tomorrow."

Sam flipped through the pages. "Anything stand out?"

"No, not really. Hidalgo's blood alcohol level was well over the legal limit. Full tox wasn't back. And the priest . . . no evidence of sexual trauma. And there's DNA from a second male in his bed."

Sam looked up and met her eyes. "This case sucks," she said quietly.

"Hunter," Malone yelled from his doorway. When Tori and

Sam both turned, he stared at them, then held open his hands.

"What the hell? We've been waiting for over an hour."

"I was at the lab."

He pointed down the hall. "Conference room. Now. Sikes? Ramirez? You too."

"Does he seem a little agitated?" Tori whispered.

"I think he's scared of her. She dissed him right in front of me and Sikes. Hell, I'm scared of her."

Malone took his seat at the head of the table. "Everyone's already been introduced. Hunter, this is Marissa Goddard, from Boston."

Marissa smiled and nodded politely at Tori. "Detective Hunter, nice to finally meet you." She looked at her watch. "You're an hour late."

Tori stared at her, then slowly shoved the sleeve away from her own watch. "Actually, I'm quite early. The lab is never this prompt with their reports. I suppose the mayor's office lit a fire under them. Shame all our victims aren't priests."

Marissa leaned forward. "We're not going to have a problem here, are we? Because I'm sensing a problem, Detective."

"Problem? The problem I have is having you in our squad room during a murder investigation."

"Hunter, chill," Malone said before quickly glancing at Sam.

Tori felt Sam's hand on her thigh, giving her a squeeze. Tori tensed for a moment, then relaxed.

Malone went on. "As I said earlier, Ms. Goddard will be involved in the details of the case. She will be speaking to the media on behalf of the diocese. The chief wants her in the know. What she does and does not tell them is of no concern of ours. Same with CIU." He looked at Hunter. "Are we clear?"

"I don't feel comfortable sharing details of a case with a civilian, Lieutenant."

"Well, the chief doesn't care what we feel comfortable with, Hunter."

"Civilian? I wouldn't exactly call myself a civilian, Detective. We're on the same team, after all."

Tori leaned forward. "People I don't know don't get to play on my team," she said evenly. "And I don't know you."

Marissa smiled. "Well, then we'll just have to rectify that, won't we." She turned to Malone. "Shall we get on with it? I have another meeting in forty-five minutes."

Lieutenant Malone took a deep breath, and Tori saw the frustration on his face. "Okay, Hunter. I've already gone over the preliminaries with her. Why don't you fill us all in on the lab reports? Did you bring copies?"

She held up a file. "I've just got my copy. Everything on Hidalgo is being sent to Sikes and Ramirez. Mac didn't have a full report from the rectory. There was a lot to process." She glanced at Marissa Goddard, whose notebook was turned at an odd angle as she wrote in the normal hook-handed position of most left-handed people. "There were thirteen usable prints from the rectory. The only one they got a hit on was Hidalgo's. His prints were on the lamp and the belt."

"And I understand strangulation by that very belt was the cause of death," Marissa stated, looking up from her notes. "Should be a fairly easy case for you, Detective."

Before Tori could respond, John sat up straight, tapping the tabletop lightly with his perfectly manicured nails. "Circumstantial evidence without a motive is not what we would call an easy case, Ms. Goddard." He smiled charmingly. "By the way, do you already have dinner plans? I'd be happy to introduce you to a good restaurant this evening."

Tori rolled her eyes and lightly bumped knees with John under the table. He never could pass up an opportunity to flirt with a pretty face, although she suspected Marissa Goddard had no interest in John Sikes.

"Thank you, Detective, but no thanks." She looked pointedly at Tori. "I read all the time about murders committed without motive. Surely that won't have a bearing on this case?"

Tori stared back into the unblinking green eyes. "The fact that there's evidence of sexual activity, a struggle, a dead suspect—yes, a lack of motive definitely has a bearing."

"Detective, I believe *alleged* sexual activity would be the proper description. And I feel confident that sexual assault will be the finding, not consensual. Let's not get ahead of ourselves here."

Tori opened the file she was holding, trying to find her notes from Jackson's post. She read aloud, "'Rectal bleeding appears to be from recent intercourse. No fluids found. There was no trauma to indicate assault.'" She looked up. "Appears to be consensual."

Marissa smiled and clasped her hands together, resting her elbows on the table. "*Appears*, Detective. That's the word you should be focusing on. Not fact, but opinion. Most likely your opinion."

"My opinion based on the findings of the M.E." Tori was no dummy. Two could play at this game.

Marissa waved her hand dismissively. "Which is why you are not speaking to the press, Detective." She smiled again. "And regardless, I'm not certain what bearing that should have on your case."

"Ms. Goddard, if Father Michael was engaged in a sexual affair, we may now have motive," Sam said. "Just because we *think* Hidalgo murdered him, just because we have circumstantial evidence to that effect, we can't close the case and state emphatically that Hidalgo was the killer."

"Besides, Hidalgo is dead," Ramirez said.

"Your dead suspect does not concern me," Marissa said.

"Apparently, your dead priest doesn't concern you much either," Tori said as she closed her file and slapped it loudly on the table. "You're more worried about damage control than finding a killer."

"I do believe finding the killer is your job, not mine."

"Exactly. That's why you don't get to be on our team, and that's why you shouldn't even be in this goddamn room!" Tori said forcefully.

Sam grabbed her thigh under the table the same instant John pressed his knee against hers.

"Hunter, I swear," Malone said with a shake of his head.

"It's okay, Lieutenant," Marissa said as she slowly stood, gathering her papers. "I've heard enough for now." Her glance traveled between Tori and Sam, then back at Sam. "Is she this passionate about everything, Samantha?"

Tori tensed, but she kept quiet as she felt Sam's grip tighten on her thigh.

"Actually, yes, she is, Ms. Goddard."

Marissa raised her eyebrows in surprise. "Well, lucky you." She stared at Tori for a moment, then pushed her chair away. At the door, she paused. "I'm not your enemy, Detective." She smiled. "Which is probably a good thing. I'm sure you have plenty already."

The door closed behind her and Sam loosened her grip on Tori's leg.

"You know, I don't think I like her very much," Sam said seriously.

The others laughed, then Malone pointed at John. "I can't believe you asked her out, Sikes. What the hell were you thinking?"

He shrugged. "She's cute."

Tori nudged him. "I don't think you're her type, John."

John leaned around Tori and pointed at Sam. "Told you so. You owe me ten bucks."

Malone cleared his throat loudly. "Can we please get back to the task at hand?" He stared at Tori. "And you. Jesus Christ,

41

Hunter, get over it already, will you. She's here to stay. I don't see the point in trying to piss her off."

"This is completely unorthodox, Lieutenant. She has no business knowing everything about our investigation."

"Don't you think I know that, Hunter? Don't you think I've already questioned it? And I was told to shut up and follow orders, which is what I'm telling you to do."

"Well, I want to know what the hell is going on. The church obviously suspects something or they wouldn't be so concerned with controlling the press. It makes no goddamn sense."

"It makes perfect sense, Tori," Sam said. "I don't like it either, but it doesn't necessarily mean they know something about Father Michael. The Dallas Diocese got dragged through the mud several years ago by that sexual abuse scandal. And then after the judge ordered that the files be made public, a lot of the attempted cover-up came out. You can't blame them for trying to protect their reputation now."

"I agree with Kennedy," Malone said. "And whether Father Michael was involved in an intimate affair or not, that's not something that needs to be made public." He looked around the room. "And we all know that eventually even the most sordid details will come out, despite their efforts to keep a lid on them. So let's don't worry about things we can't control. I'm more interested in where we are with this case."

Tori sighed. "Mac found epithelia from two sources on the sheets in Father Michael's bedroom. One was from Father Michael." She stared at Malone. "The other, unknown male."

Malone drummed his fingers slowly on the tabletop as he stared at the ceiling. "Goddamn. Well, okay then. I guess I need to quit assuming Father Michael was a saint," he said quietly. "Damn. I was really hoping—"

"I'm sorry, Stan," Tori said.

"Yeah, well, I wanted to think it was assault just like Ms. Goddard there." He cleared his throat. "And, Hunter, just because you kept this bit of information from her, don't think she won't find out about it. I'm fairly certain she's on the list of persons to receive copies of the reports."

Frustrated, Tori shook her head. "Which is another reason she has no business being here. She'll already knows as much as we do. Probably more."

"That goes without saying. Okay, back to this. So we'll go with a sexual partner." Malone looked around the room. "How do we find him?"

"Thirteen sets of prints. One of them has got to be his," John said.

"That's providing the diocese will let us print their priests so we can match them. And I wouldn't hold your breath on that," Tori said.

"I think there's an easier way," Sam said. "The housekeeper. I think we need to pay her another visit."

"She was shocked when I asked her that question, Sam," Tori reminded her. "In fact, I think she was insulted."

"Yeah. Maybe she was too shocked. I mean, if anyone would know about an affair, it would be the housekeeper."

CHAPTER SEVEN

"Did she mean what I thought she meant?" Sam asked Tori later that evening as they sat curled together on the sofa watching TV.

"Hmm?"

"Goddard. When she asked if you were passionate. Was she insinuating something?"

Tori chuckled. "Yeah. I'd say she was insinuating."

Sam hit the mute button on the remote. "Do you think she's gay?" she asked quietly, as if someone might overhear her question.

Tori gave a wry smile. "Did you pay John the ten bucks you owed him for the bet?"

Sam kissed Tori on the lips. "There's nothing about her that would make me think she's gay. How do you know?"

"The same reason she knew about us."

"In other words, there's no reason. You just know."

"Yeah. You just know."

"Do you think she'll be a problem?"

"About us or about this case?"

Nervous about being outed, Sam sighed. "Both, I guess."

"I think it's just crazy that she's even here. A consulting firm? For a murder? It makes no sense."

"I guess they're just trying to cover their bases. Put a positive spin on things before the media turns it into something ugly." Sam stood, heading to the kitchen. "Want more wine?"

"Sure. And it makes them look guilty." Tori pointed at the TV. "And her little speech on the news tonight was just bullshit. 'Preserve the sanctity'? What is she trying to do?"

Sam smiled as she returned with the wine bottle, still a bit surprised at the instant animosity between Tori and Marissa Goddard. Of course, she shouldn't be. Tori was never one to embrace strangers, never one to trust without cause.

"What? You think I'm being ridiculous?" Tori asked.

Sam wrapped her fingers around Tori's arm and squeezed lightly. "No, sweetheart, not at all."

Tori laughed. "You do, don't you?"

"Oh, not ridiculous. I just think it's a waste of time to dwell on it. As Malone said, she's here whether we like it or not. We still have to do our job."

Tori met her eyes, smiling. "Yeah. But she's obnoxious as hell."

CHAPTER EIGHT

"Is this the place?"

Sam looked at her notes, then nodded. "Yeah." She pointed to an old blue truck. "Park there."

Tori pulled to the curb behind the truck, looking around Sam to the red brick, ranch-style home, much like all the others on the block. Years and years ago, this part of Dallas was probably considered an upscale neighborhood. Now—with the leaves gone from the trees, the grass turned a winter brown, the paint faded and chipped along the eaves—the houses looked old and worn. She imagined Alice Hagen's husband wasn't able to do much around the house. She'd said he had emphysema.

Tori grabbed Sam's arm, stopping her from opening her door. "You do the talking," she said. "I'm not good with this stuff."

Sam smiled. "Of course. Although this will be my first time to accuse a priest of having an affair."

They got out and Tori said, "Yeah. But you'll do it much more diplomatically than I would." Tori paused at the front door, glancing at the flowerpots, the plants dead and brown, victims of the frost they'd had a couple of weeks ago.

"Kinda unkempt," Sam said. "After meeting with her—and her being a housekeeper—I would have expected something more pristine."

"Detective, are you being judgmental or just observant?"

"Maybe just stereotyping." Sam pushed the doorbell. "And just for the record, I'm not looking forward to this."

Tori leaned closer, her mouth just inches from Sam's ear. "Don't worry. I've got your back."

Just then the door cracked open. Sam smiled pleasantly at Alice Hagen. "Mrs. Hagen, so sorry to intrude on you like this, but we have a few more questions." She gestured at Tori. "You remember Detective Hunter?"

Tori nodded politely, trying to ignore the suspicious look the older woman gave her. She waited as Alice Hagen looked them over from behind the door before opening it fully.

"Of course. What can I do for you?"

"May we come in?" Sam asked.

Mrs. Hagen glanced over her shoulder back down the dark hallway before nodding. "Okay. But my husband—"

"We'll only take a few moments of your time," Tori interrupted.

"Well, come into the kitchen then." She stepped aside. "He's in the den watching television."

They followed her into the house, both pausing while she closed the door behind them. Tori noted the difference between the inside of the home and the outside. Here, there was no clutter, no disorder. She glanced at the framed photos hanging on the wall, thinking the Hagens must have a large family. She quickly counted more than ten family portraits. Sam was looking at them too, and Tori watched as Sam's gaze left the portraits and

47

landed on her.

The kitchen was big and airy, the blinds all opened to let in the first rays of sunshine they'd seen in a week. In the center of the small breakfast table was a vase stuffed full of fresh flowers. Again, not a thing looked out of place.

"I can make a fresh pot of coffee, if you'd like," Alice offered.

"Oh, no, Mrs. Hagen, we don't want you to go to any trouble," Sam said. She gave another friendly smile. "I noticed the pictures in the hallway. You have a big family?"

"Sit, please," Alice said, motioning to the table and chairs. "We have six children and they've blessed us with seventeen grandchildren." A hint of pride flashed in her eyes. "It's quite a houseful at Christmas, yes."

Tori shifted impatiently and glanced at Sam, wishing they'd just get on with it. Pleasantries were one thing, but they had a dead priest to deal with.

Sam gave her a subtle touch on the shoulder as she moved behind her to the far chair. "Well, Mrs. Hagen, again I'm sorry to drop by unannounced, but we've got a few more questions about Father Michael."

"I don't understand. They said on the news this morning that Juan did it." She shook her head. "Never would have believed it. Juan was always so polite, so grateful to have a job. Why, he'd do anything for Father Michael. And now him being killed himself. Why, it's just awful."

Tori and Sam exchanged glances. Tori frowned. News? What news? They hadn't heard anything, but they hadn't bothered with the TV this morning.

"Excuse me, but we've not made any formal charges yet," Tori said. "Juan Hidalgo is simply a suspect at this point."

"But that woman said—"

"What woman?" Tori said sharply.

"Well, the one they interviewed. That cute newswoman on Channel Five—Melissa Carter—talked with her this morning.

She was at the church."

Tori reached for her cell. "Goddamn," she said under her breath, but Sam stopped her with a quick touch on her arm.

"We're just following up on some leads, Mrs. Hagen. We're not convinced Juan did it," Sam said easily. "I'm sure you wouldn't want us to rush to judgment and accuse an innocent man."

"Of course not, no."

"Good. Now tell us a little about Father Michael. He was obviously well-liked. Was there anyone who he may have had stay overnight with him? Or someone who spent a lot of time there at the rectory?"

Mrs. Hagen fidgeted, her hands clasping and unclasping in her lap, but she shook her head. "No. There was no one."

Tori sat back and let Sam take over. It was, she reasoned, what Sam excelled at. Tori had no patience when it came to questions.

"The rectory was large, at least three bedrooms. Was Father Michael the only one who lived there?" Sam asked.

"Yes. Well, at times, visiting priests would stay, priests from other parishes. But none of the other priests from Saint Mary's lived there."

"How did Father Michael come to live there?"

"What do you mean?"

"Well, he wasn't the oldest, didn't have the most tenure. Why was he given the rectory to live in and not another priest?"

Mrs. Hagen fingered the buttons on her blue housedress. "I don't know about that, but there are other houses. The church owns nearly all of the buildings in the surrounding blocks."

"Okay, so other priests have their own homes?"

"Some share houses, yes. Saint Mary's is a large parish, Detective. Plus, when priests leave the seminary, some stay on here for a few months or so, before they're assigned to another parish. And of course St. Iglesias has three priests that live at Saint Mary's too."

Sam paused, her eyes flicking toward Tori, and Tori wondered how much longer she would be able to sit idly by before demanding to know who shared Father Michael's bed. She took a deep breath, willing herself to keep quiet.

"Mrs. Hagen, but you're sure no one lived with Father Michael?"

"I'm his housekeeper. I guess I'd know, wouldn't I?"

Tori had had it. She stood quickly, pushing her chair back, and looked from Alice Hagen to Sam. Hands on her hips, she stared at Mrs. Hagen. "You're the housekeeper, right. Which is why we're asking these questions. I know it must be difficult for you, having to discuss Father Michael's private life, especially since he's not here to defend himself. But if we're going to find out who killed him and why, we're going to need to know who he was—"

"Mrs. Hagen, please." Sam's smile was apologetic. "We're not here to judge him, and we're not here to make false accusations, but the evidence tells us that there was a possibility he was physically involved with another man. Please, if you know anything, you need to tell us," she said gently.

But the housekeeper shook her head, glancing with frightened eyes at Tori and Sam before averting her gaze. "I told you, I don't know anything about that. Father Michael was a wonderful man, a wonderful priest," she said, quickly dabbing tears that slid down her cheeks. "I can't believe you are accusing him of such a thing. He was a *priest*. Have you no shame?"

Fed up, Tori went back to the table, her hands gripping the back of the chair as she gave a heavy, exaggerated sigh. "Mrs. Hagen, we have no idea why Father Michael was killed. As you said, he was a wonderful person. Who would want to kill him? Why?" She leaned closer. The woman was obviously lying. "Someone shared his bed, Mrs. Hagen. DNA evidence tells us that. We need to know who it was."

Mrs. Hagen's hands trembled as she stood. It was then that

Tori noticed the rosary beads in her palm.

"I'd like for you to leave now, Detectives. I have nothing more to say."

"Mrs. Hagen—"

"Detective Kennedy, we've taken enough of her time," Tori said. "Let's get back to the station."

Sam opened her mouth as if to ask one more question of Mrs. Hagen, but the older woman looked away. Tori led the way out of the house. On the front steps they looked at each other.

Sam must have noted Tori's skepticism because she said, "I think she's lying. You think she's lying, right?"

"I'd say. Did you see how she was worrying those rosary beads?" Tori headed down the steps. "We need to find out what the hell Marissa Goddard said on the news this morning."

CHAPTER NINE

Sikes, Ramirez and Malone were huddled together, Sikes with his ear to a phone, when Tori and Sam came into the squad room.

"This can't be good," Sam said.

Tori's cell rang. "Hunter," she answered in the same instant she tapped John on the shoulder.

John jumped, then slammed his phone down. "Goddamn, Hunter, you scared the shit out of me."

"You rang?"

"We were just about to head out. Got tox back on Hidalgo. He was juiced. And not just the alcohol. Cocaine and meth."

Tori raised her eyebrows. "And?"

"Tony talked to his mother this morning. And to Hector Ybarro. He was the one who found the body."

"Yes, I remember him."

"According to them, Hidalgo was clean. Hadn't touched drugs in over a year, and hardly ever drank more than a beer or two. In fact, he was so clean, he was able to hold two jobs. Besides working at the church, he was also the maintenance man at his apartment building."

"So then what are you thinking? He went on a binge, lost his mind and killed Father Michael?"

"Actually, we were thinking the opposite," Ramirez said. "Killed Father Michael, then was so distraught, he went on a binge."

"So we still don't know why he would have killed him."

"Ybarro gave us the name of a couple of bars in Little Mexico where Hidalgo used to hang out. We're going to go see if Juan hit any of them that morning."

"Sounds good. Let me know what you find." Tori looked at Malone. "We didn't get shit from the housekeeper, by the way."

"I take it you haven't seen the paper this morning." He pointed to her desk where the *Dallas Morning News* lay. "Goddard is in town one day and makes the front page."

"Mrs. Hagen said she saw on the news where the murder was solved," Sam said. "Did we miss something? Or has CIU closed the case?"

"As I was told this morning by the chief, Goddard is speaking on behalf of the diocese only. Basically, she *implied* the case was closed and that Juan Hidalgo was the murderer."

"Did she also imply that Hidalgo was now dead?" Sam asked.

Malone shook his head. "I've been thinking. We've gone over all these scenarios, but we haven't even considered that the two murders are simply random and unrelated."

Tori tossed the paper back on her desk, her eyes finding Sam's before staring at the lieutenant. "Are you seriously considering that? Come on, Lieutenant, we've been in this business long enough to not believe in coincidences."

"True. I'm just saying it's a possibility and we shouldn't rule it out altogether."

"As a last resort," Tori said. "Now, what's Goddard's phone number? Does anyone have it?"

"I have it, yes," Sam said. "Why?"

"Because we've got thirteen prints to account for." She took the business card Sam handed her. "I think we need to pay the diocese a visit."

"Will you quit fidgeting," Sam whispered, watching as Tori paced back and forth across the plush carpet.

Tori shoved her hands into her pockets, her eyes darting around the large room. Sam followed her gaze, admiring the religious oil paintings that adorned the walls. Probably 19th century, she thought.

"What is wrong with you?"

Tori took her hands out of her pockets and tucked them under her arms. "This place gives me the creeps," she said softly. "It's too damn quiet."

Sam smiled. "We're at a church."

"Yeah, well, we're not *in* the church. Why is everything so . . . so solemn?" She looked around again. "So *formal*."

"Why, Detective Hunter, are you feeling out of place?" Sam teased.

Tori again shoved her hands in the pockets of her jeans. "Maybe I'm scared of those lightning bolts Sikes was talking about."

Sam knew, even though Tori was teasing, a little part of her was quite scared to be here. But she doubted a stranger would recognize that from Tori's body language. Pressed jeans today with a dark burgundy sweater pulled over an equally pressed shirt, her short dark hair as neat as ever—Tori exuded nothing but confidence. In fact, she positively oozed it. It was one of those things about Tori Hunter that still amazed Sam. No matter the circumstance, no matter the situation, no matter the people involved, Tori would take control and never relinquish the power.

She smiled slightly as she met Tori's eyes. She suspected that Marissa Goddard was as used to being in control as Tori was. And the power struggle they were having, while amusing, wasn't really helping their investigation any.

"I doubt God will take His wrath out on you with lightning bolts," she whispered.

"Oh? Something worse?"

Sam laughed. "What? You think because we're accusing a priest of having an affair, that warrants retaliation?"

Clearly amused, Tori raised an eyebrow. "Perhaps our punishment is having to deal with Marissa Goddard."

They both looked up at the sound of heels clicking methodically on the marble hallway leading to the reception room they'd been placed in. Marissa Goddard, in her black business suit and smart red blouse, looked, Sam thought, positively regal as she approached them.

"Detectives, what an absolute pleasure," she said with a hint of sarcasm. "I expected you hours ago."

"Sorry. We missed your morning news debut or we would have hopped right over," Tori said, equally as sarcastic. "I hear you've solved the case for us."

Marissa smirked. "Just prodding you along. With all the evidence, it seems obvious Hidalgo is your killer."

"Circumstantial evidence without a motive is hardly conclusive, Ms. Goddard. I thought we'd already established that." Tori squared her shoulders, waiting.

"Had we?" Marissa turned to admire a painting of the Virgin Mary. "The artwork in here is exquisite," she murmured, glancing back to them. "Do either of you know art?"

"Not really, no," Sam said. "But they are very beautiful."

Tori cleared her throat. "Can we forego the pleasantries,

please? We're here on business."

"I wasn't aware you were being pleasant, Detective. I assumed that was a trait you didn't possess." She smiled at Sam. "Although your record with partners seems to have improved now that Detective Kennedy is on board." At Tori's blank stare, Marissa continued. "Yes, I've seen your file, Detective Hunter. Quite impressive. Quite *scary*, in fact."

Tori raised an eyebrow. "Thanks. How many privacy acts did you violate to get a look at my file?" She shrugged. "But it doesn't matter. My file is hardly relevant to our case. Thirteen sets of fingerprints are. We want to print the priests here at Saint Mary's. The priests in the seminary. Any nuns that might have had cause to be in the rectory. Anyone else, for that matter, who may have been in the rectory."

Marissa Goddard chortled. "Are you out of your mind?"

"I don't think so, no," Tori said. "Why? Is that a problem?"

"I suppose you think you can get a court order for this?"

"Why would that be necessary? I would think the church would be anxious to find Father Michael's killer, not hinder a police investigation by refusing to cooperate."

Marissa laughed. "Are you serious? You would accuse the church of not cooperating?"

"As if it has something to hide? Yes."

"Hide? Are you going to start all that *sexual partner* garbage again, Hunter?"

Sam watched Tori, wondering if she should intervene before this got out of hand.

Tori closed the space between her and Marissa. "Don't think I won't talk to the media."

"Oh, Detective Hunter, don't you even presume to threaten me," she said with a snide smile. "I'd hate to pull rank on you."

Tori frowned. "Pull rank?"

"I had dinner with the police chief last evening, as well as the mayor. Both fine gentlemen. You do know I'm here at their request, don't you?"

Tori sighed. "Goddamn politics. Does the church have incriminating pictures of our city's leaders or what?" She leaned closer. "What in the world could they be trying to hide, I wonder? I thought all of their skeletons were already exposed."

"I assure you, they have nothing to hide, Detective. They simply don't want a media circus surrounding this investigation. Father Michael deserves to be laid to rest in peace."

"I agree. He also deserves justice."

"And someone took care of that, didn't he? Hidalgo is dead."

Sam had had enough. They were getting nothing accomplished this way. "Ms. Goddard, that's hardly justice," Sam said. "We don't know for sure Hidalgo did it. And if he did, we certainly don't know why."

"Does it really matter at this point? And please, call me Marissa."

"Of course. But yes, it matters."

"Look, I'm tired of all these games already, Goddard. We need prints," Tori said again. "So go talk to whoever it is you need to talk to."

Marissa put her hands on her hips, looking from Sam to Tori and back to Sam. "God, how do you put up with her?" she murmured before striding away, her stilettos echoing on the marble floor. "I'll talk to the monsignor. Don't hold your breath."

"Thanks. We'll just wait here," Tori called after her.

Sam watched her disappear down the hall, then turned to Tori. "I wonder if, under other circumstances, we might be friends with her. You think?"

"Are you kidding? She's abrasive. She's opinionated. Jesus, who could stand to be around her?"

Sam laughed. "I think that's the way Sikes described you when I first started working with you guys."

"He did, huh?" Tori shrugged. "Well, I guess it was true, right?"

Sam moved closer, her hand snaking between them to rest at Tori's waist. "It *was* true, sweetheart. And I fell in love with you anyway," she whispered. She caught the gentle softening of Tori's eyes, the soft blush that crept across her flawless skin.

Tori nodded. "I was abrasive, wasn't I?"

Sam laughed again. "Unbearable."

Tori went to inspect the same painting Marissa Goddard had studied earlier. She turned around slowly. "It's a little ironic, don't you think? That they have a woman as the consultant for the church," she explained.

"I suppose."

"I mean, the Catholic Church is all about men. Women are simply—"

"What? Subservient? Obedient?" Sam asked, her lips twitching as she tried not to smile at Tori's musings.

"Yeah. They have no power. Why in the world would they have a woman as their spokesperson?"

"Well, in the public's eye, a woman is more sympathetic, more honest." Sam raised her eyebrows. "More believable."

"Yeah. And I guess that's a good thing when you're lying to them."

Sam hadn't thought of that. "You don't think she was brought here for that reason, do you?"

Tori's reply was cut short as Marissa Goddard reappeared.

"Well, you caught him on a good day. Monsignor Bernard has agreed to see you."

"Why, thank you, Ms. Goddard, you are even more powerful than I suspected," Tori said lightly as they followed her down the hall.

"Trust me, Hunter, I advised him to send you on your merry way and make you beg for a court order. But he insists that we cooperate in any way." Marissa smiled. "And don't get your hopes up on the fingerprints. I don't think he's too keen on that."

Sam watched the exchange with amusement. Again, she

couldn't understand their animosity. Granted, Marissa Goddard was a bit brusque and uncompromising, but still, she wasn't the most detestable person to work with. In fact, she seemed to have quite the sense of humor, even if it was mostly at their expense.

"Marissa, if I may ask," Sam said, "how long have you been consulting for the church?"

"You remember several years ago when they had all that mess in Boston? The diocese there hired the firm I work for to oversee newspaper and TV. It was a total nightmare." She paused at a door, a massive oak structure with detailed carvings etched into the wood. "But they took a liking to me and thought I handled the media well." She smiled confidently. "Which is why I'm here."

She knocked once before opening the door. Sam watched Tori as Tori moved into the room, her gaze landing on Monsignor Bernard. His mahogany desk, Sam thought, was impressive.

"Come in, Detectives." He pointed to the plush leather chairs sitting opposite his desk. "Please, have a seat."

"Thank you for seeing us, Monsignor," Sam said politely as she moved around Tori to one of the chairs.

"Of course. As I told Ms. Goddard, we're here to help in any way." He nodded at Tori as he pulled open a drawer. "Detective Hunter, a pleasure to see you again."

Marissa strolled nonchalantly into the room, claiming the sofa on the far wall. Tori finally took a seat next to Sam and nodded casually at the monsignor, watching as he methodically opened a tube of lotion and squirted a small glob into his palm.

"This weather wrecks havoc on my skin," he said, rubbing the lotion onto his hands.

"I appreciate you taking the time to visit with us, Monsignor Bernard. I'm assuming Ms. Goddard shared our request with you," Tori said, her tone a bit abrupt, even for her.

"You have a request, Detective? No, she said you had some

questions." He dropped the tube of lotion back into his drawer, waiting.

Tori gave Marissa a humorless smile, which she returned in kind. "The killer was obviously in the rectory. We have recovered thirteen different fingerprints from the scene. We would like to identify those thirteen."

He folded his hands together on his desk, his plump fingers twitching lightly against the backs of his now smooth hands, his eyes thoughtful as he eyed them. "I see. But I am curious as to why. If Juan killed Father Michael, why are you concerned with who else may have been in the rectory? For example, I'm sure one of those prints will be mine. I visit the rectory quite often."

"Monsignor, we have not determined for certain that Juan was the killer," Sam said.

Evidently surprised, he glanced at Marissa. "I'm sorry. I was under the impression that the evidence pointed to Juan."

"Circumstantial evidence at best," Tori said. "And without a motive," she added. "It's a little hard to close the case."

"Which is why we'd like to identify the prints and interview everyone," Sam said.

"Well, I'm shocked, Detectives. You actually think someone from Saint Mary's could be the killer? Why, any of the prints you find in the rectory would have a legitimate reason for being there."

"Which is fine," Tori said. "But we'd like to account for everyone. That's our job."

"I just don't feel comfortable subjecting my people to this, Detective. It's as if you're putting them in a lineup, assuming one of them is guilty."

"Hardly. But we can't investigate this case without knowing who the players are."

"In this day of forensic evidence, you're telling me you have something more concrete than what points to Juan Hidalgo? There has to be some reason you're curious about the prints," he said. "I won't allow a witch hunt here, Detective. I'm well aware of your opinion regarding Father Michael's . . . *personal* . . . life."

"Monsignor, we'd just like to interview everyone who may have had contact with Father Michael," Sam said. "There has to be a reason he was murdered. Aren't you anxious to know why?"

"I'm anxious to put this whole thing behind us and move on. We have news vans parked across the street daily, the phone rings constantly, the parishioners are upset. Father Michael was very popular among them. He was young, vibrant, full of ideas. I'd just like to bring closure to his life, to honor him and to lay him to rest."

"And you won't be able to do that until we know his killer," Tori said evenly.

"I still don't like the idea of interrogating my people. They have the same rights as anyone else. I don't believe you have a basis to invade their privacy this way. It makes me think you're searching for something else, Detective Hunter, some potential scandal you can bring to light."

Tori glared at him. No doubt she was long weary of this inane conversation, which in Sam's opinion was going nowhere. "Given the circumstances, I don't see us getting a court order, or so Ms. Goddard claims." She turned to look at Marissa. "Apparently she's got some inside information from the chief." She turned back to the monsignor. "So I'm to assume from your statements then that you don't care about your murdered priest. You're more concerned about protecting the privacy of the church and protecting the goddamn reputation of this diocese." Her voice rose. "What are you afraid we'll find?"

Sam's eyes widened at Tori's outburst and she just barely resisted the urge to grasp her arm, trying to calm her. She stared at the monsignor, his plump face red with anger.

"Detective Hunter, if you *ever* speak to me like that again, I will have you removed from these premises and barred from returning. I have never been spoken to so discourteously in all my life." His palm slapped down on the top of the desk loudly. "Have you no respect?"

At this, Sam did grab Tori's arm before the situation got any worse. "Monsignor, I apologize for her," she said quickly, chancing a quick glance at Tori. "We're just very frustrated. We're at a standstill, basically, unless you help us. I understand you're trying to preserve the reputation of your church, but a man has been murdered. A priest. *Your* priest. And we want to find his killer."

He glared at them, his breathing labored as he attempted to regain his composure. He took a deep breath, finally nodding at Sam. "Ms. Goddard tells me your brother is a priest." He covered his mouth as he coughed lightly. "What diocese?"

Sam looked quickly at Marissa, surprised at how thorough she'd been in her background investigation. Actually, it was interesting she'd even done a background check to begin with.

"We're from Denver originally," Sam said. "He volunteered for South America as soon as he got out of the seminary. He's been in Brazil for years."

"Wonderful. A man of conviction. I spent five years in Nicaragua myself. It will test your faith down there, that's for certain. You must be very proud of him."

She smiled at Monsignor Bernard. "Yes. My parents are especially proud."

"Very well." He nodded before leaning his head back against his leather chair, his eyes closing as he appeared deep in thought. Or prayer.

Sam glanced at Tori, thankful she seemed to have gotten herself under control, then at Marissa. Marissa met her gaze without expression, then turned her attention back to the monsignor.

"Very well," he said again, this time softly, as if to himself. He leaned forward, his forearms resting on his desk. "I shall honor your request, Detective Kennedy. I'll have Sister Margaret give me a list of her charges who may have had reason to be in the rectory. I'll also get a list of the other priests and seminarians. I'll have Ms. Goddard get you their names."

"Excuse me, Monsignor, but I don't think this is a good idea," Marissa said, speaking for the first time. "It's not our responsibility to—"

"Good idea or not, it's what we'll do," he said. "The sooner they complete this investigation, the sooner we can return to normal. I don't expect they'll find anything out of the ordinary." He looked pointedly at Sam. "But be advised, I won't force them to comply with anything. We are still citizens and therefore afforded the same rights as citizens. If they don't feel comfortable giving their fingerprints to the police department," he said, "that is their choice."

"Of course, Monsignor. We understand." If that was the case, Sam thought, they'd have to work to get a warrant. The prints were the only thing they had to go on at this point.

"Good. Now, if you'll excuse me, I have other business to attend to."

They stood, and Sam nudged Tori with her elbow, hoping she'd apologize to him. But Tori's pronounced frown and set jaw told her she would not get her wish.

"Thank you, Monsignor," Sam said politely.

"I'll show you out," Marissa offered as she held open the heavy door.

But Sam had a thought and turned around to face him again. "If I may ask, how did Father Michael come to live at the rectory?"

"Excuse me?"

"I mean, why was he allowed to live there and not another priest?"

He pursed his lips. "Oh. You want to know the pecking order?"

Sam nodded.

"As with any business, the most productive are often

rewarded," he said. "Father Michael was very popular, as I said. He was also our most gifted priest when it came to soliciting charitable contributions."

"You mean he collected more money than anyone else?"

"Exactly. It's a competition most of them have come to enjoy, I believe. And the reward is getting to live alone at the rectory, along with having a housekeeper and cook."

"I see. Well, thank you again, Monsignor."

CHAPTER TEN

"Oh, hell no," Tori said as they explained to Lieutenant Malone how it went with the monsignor. She took a swig from her water bottle, drinking nearly half of it. "I blew up at him, but Sam saved the day."

"Saying *goddamn* to a Catholic priest is a little more than blowing up at him, Hunter," Sam said with a laugh. "I'm surprised those lightning bolts you've been expecting didn't hit at that particular moment."

"Well, at least you got what you went after. Sikes and Ramirez got something too. They're on their way back. We'll meet in my office." Malone held up two files. "By the way, I'm pulling these. One is your homeless guy. I'm giving it to Donaldson."

"Donaldson?" Tori looked around, noting that Donaldson and his partner were out. "Lieutenant, you know how I feel about him. Ever since they went cold on—"

"Hunter, you know it was Adams and not Donaldson, so cut him some slack. He's had enough shit from Internal Affairs, he doesn't need it from his own squad."

"Yeah. But our homeless guy?"

"How much time have you spent on it in the last three days?"

"He's right, Tori," Sam said. "We've got our hands full. Besides, Donaldson's anxious to show you—all of us—that he's a good detective. He'll do a first-rate job."

Tori stared at her, knowing it was true. "You're right. Okay," she said, nodding at Malone.

Malone grinned. "Thanks, Hunter, but I don't really care if you okay it or not. It's a done deal," he said as he headed back to his office.

"You know, in the past, he *would* care if I said it was okay or not." Tori frowned, wondering if she'd lost her edge. "What's up with that?"

Sam burst out laughing. "Perhaps it's because you've mellowed and he's no longer afraid you'll pull your weapon and shoot him," Sam teased.

"Mellowed," Tori muttered, disgusted at the notion. "I haven't mellowed. I don't know what you're talking about."

Sam's eyes were twinkling as she leaned closer. "Do you have any idea how much I love you?"

Tori's breath caught, much like it did every time Sam uttered those words to her. Words she still, on occasion, had a hard time believing. But whenever she looked into Sam's eyes, the doubt always left her. She closed her own for a second, and then said begrudgingly, "Maybe I have . . . mellowed."

"If it's any consolation, you're still a total bitch out in the field."

"Well, thanks, Detective. That's the best compliment you could have given me."

"Yes, I know."

"What compliment?" Sikes asked as he and Ramirez walked past.

"I called her a bitch," Sam offered.

"Oh. So nothing new." He didn't stop at his desk but kept walking to Malone's office. "Come on. I think Malone wants us all in on this."

They got up to follow him, Tori nudging Ramirez on the arm as they went in. "You get something good?"

"Yeah. Think so."

"Sit. Sit. Let's get on with it," Malone said. "I've got to meet with the captain at three. I'd like to have something to tell him." He pointed at Sikes. "What'd you find out?"

"I'll let Tony tell you. My Spanish isn't that great."

"Yeah, we went down to Little Mexico," Tony explained. "A bar called La Sombra. It means like . . . in the shadows." He looked at his notes. "Hidalgo showed up the morning of the murder around eight. He was drinking tequila straight up."

"Wait a minute. This bar is open for business at eight in the morning?" Sam asked.

"I kinda got the impression they never closed," Ramirez said. "Anyway, Hidalgo hadn't been in the place in over a year. He stayed until two, when he scored a hit from someone." He looked up. "No names. Sorry."

"We're not trying to do a drug bust. Go on," Malone said.

"He left with some guy who was supposed to give him a ride home. And listen to this. Carlos, the bartender we talked to, said Juan kept going on about burning in hell for what he did. Carlos said he had the eyes of a dead man."

"What the hell does that mean?"

"He sold his soul to the devil," Ramirez said.

"He confessed to this guy?" Sam asked.

Sikes jumped in. "Yeah. He told this guy he was ordered by God to kill Father Michael." He shrugged. "Then he found out it wasn't really God who told him. Whatever the hell that means."

Malone rubbed his forehead, shaking his head. "That's what you got? God told him to do it?" He stared at them. "That's what you want me to go to the captain with? *God?*"

"How hard would it be to get names?" Tori asked. "Like the guy who gave him a ride?"

Tony shook his head. "No way. Just the fact that we were there asking questions today was enough. That guy's long gone. I wouldn't doubt if Carlos, our bartender, is gone too."

Malone sighed. "Okay. We got circumstantial evidence pointing to Hidalgo. Now we got what you guys say is a confession. Is that how you want to close this case?"

"Wait a minute," Tori said. "Close it? If Hidalgo *is* the killer, then who told him to kill Father Michael?"

"You think someone really told him to kill Father Michael?" Malone seemed skeptical.

"Yeah. I just don't think it was God." Tori stood, slowly pacing the room, thinking. "That would account for our lack of motive. Juan wouldn't, on his own, have a motive to kill him. But someone obviously wanted Father Michael dead. Maybe someone who also knew that Juan had a record, maybe someone who could threaten him, blackmail him."

"But who would want Father Michael dead? And why? I mean, it's not like priests make a lot of enemies," Sam said. "At least I don't think they do."

"I think we're all forgetting one thing," Sikes said. "Hidalgo is dead."

Tori nodded. "Yeah. He's dead. Who killed him? The same guy who ordered the hit on Father Michael?"

"If this guy is brave enough to whack Hidalgo, why not just kill the priest yourself? Why involve a third party?" Ramirez asked.

Tori thought for a moment. "Maybe there wasn't opportunity."

"Or maybe he just had less qualms about killing Hidalgo than killing a priest," Sikes said.

"Okay, hang on," Malone said. "You guys are talking in circles here. What if, what if. That means nothing. Facts mean something. What the hell are the facts?"

"You know, this may sound crazy," Sam said, "but could a competition between priests result in enough hate to lead to murder?"

"What are you talking about?" Sikes asked.

"Monsignor Bernard said the reason Father Michael got to live at the rectory was because he collected the most money," Sam replied. "That was his reward. You don't think one of the other priests got pissed off, do you?"

"Because of living arrangements? Pissed off enough to kill him? No. I think this still has something to do with Father Michael and his sex life," Tori said, glancing at Malone. "We got the okay to interview priests. We're going to get a chance to print them, so we can match the prints Mac found in the rectory. Let's see who was in there. Something has got to turn up."

"And I think maybe we should make an appearance at the funeral tomorrow," Sam said. "I'd like to observe everyone. If our killer is there, he might tip his hand somehow."

"I don't know if I like that," Malone said. "I don't want to turn his funeral into a circus. There'll be enough media there already. Do we really want a police presence?"

Sam smiled charmingly. "Lieutenant, I'll dress up in my Sunday best. I'll fit right in."

CHAPTER ELEVEN

Sam's heels clicked on the pavement as she crossed the street and made her way to Saint Mary's. She'd chosen her navy-blue heels to match the navy suit. She added a red blouse for a splash of color. She smiled as she remembered Tori's half-hearted offer to join her.

Tori had been standing naked in their bathroom, trying to think of an outfit she owned that would be suitable to wear to a funeral. "Those black jeans are newly pressed."

"You can't wear jeans to a funeral." Sam picked out a pair of simple gold hoops, replacing the small diamond studs she normally wore.

"I've got those khakis," she said. "And that cute silk blouse you bought me."

"It's January," Sam reminded her. "And you can't wear khakis to a funeral."

"There are far too many rules regarding clothing," Tori said, but Sam had seen the relief on her face.

Now Sam paused at the bottom of the steps leading to the church, noting the large crowd that had already gathered, nearly an hour before the service. She also noted the news vans lining the streets. But her hesitation had little to do with that.

It had been years since she'd been to Mass, the last time at her grandmother's funeral, seven years ago now. She no longer considered herself to be Catholic. In fact, she hadn't been a regular churchgoer since she lived at her parent's house. *You're here as a detective*, she chided herself. *Not a mourner*.

But still she hesitated, reluctant to take the final steps that would lead her through the open doors and into the somewhat imposing vestibule of Saint Mary's Cathedral.

"Problem, Detective?"

Sam turned, surprised at the relief she felt in seeing a familiar face, even if it was that of Marissa Goddard. She smiled, embarrassed to have been caught staring at the church as if she was afraid to enter. But in Marissa's eyes, she saw a bit of understanding.

"I was raised Catholic too," Marissa said. "But I have so many issues with the Church now, I couldn't even begin to list them all," she said with a friendly smile. "I try not to let all of their rituals and rites bother me."

"I had almost convinced myself to turn around and leave."

"I doubt they'll single you out at Mass today for being a lesbian," Marissa teased. "Come on, you can sit with me."

"Thanks," Sam said as she followed Marissa up the steps.

"Where's your partner?"

Sam looked at the cloudless sky. "She's not where she'd like to be on a warm sunny day in January, which is out on the lake fishing. That is, if she could sneak away from work," she added with a smile. "She's hanging out with Sikes and Ramirez. Getting her to come here was not really an option."

"Not surprising. I was having a hard time picturing her in a dress and heels," Marissa said with a laugh.

"Trust me, Tori Hunter does not own a dress—nor do I anticipate her ever buying one." They stopped at the entrance, the line slowing as the parishioners waited to view the body and say their final farewell to Father Michael. "And just how much research did you do on us?"

"Enough to know you wouldn't be easily swayed, which is why I insisted you not speak to the press," she said. "But I learned it is common knowledge that you and Hunter live together and all."

"Common knowledge in my squad, yes."

"No. Common knowledge on the force."

Sam shook her head. "I find that hard to believe. I doubt they would continue to let us work together if that were the case."

"Actually, I think that's about to change."

"What do you mean?" Sam asked sharply.

Marissa smiled, but shook her head. "I trust you got the list of names that Monsignor Bernard provided?"

"Yes. The crime lab will be contacting them for prints." But Sam wasn't interested in discussing fingerprints. She stopped Marissa with a hand on the arm. "What did you mean, things are about to change?"

"I'm sorry, Samantha. I shouldn't have said anything. I just got the impression in one of my meetings that you and Tori are going to be split up."

Sam stared at her. "I can't believe that. Despite our personal relationship, we work well together as partners. Tori can be a bit overbearing at times," she acknowledged. "She needs someone to offset that." She took a deep breath. She couldn't *believe* they were going to split them up. Not with Tori's track record with partners. They couldn't.

"I agree. And I know she allows you to do that. Unfortunately, her history indicates that she's never let anyone

72

do it before."

"She doesn't trust a lot of people."

Marissa led her away from the line. "This way. I assume you're here to watch. I can be of some assistance with that." They headed down a corridor and through a closed door, leaving the soft sounds of the organ music behind. From there, a flight of stairs took them to a room with a glass wall, allowing a view of the church below. The old wooden floor creaked under their weight as they entered. "I'm told this is the old cry room," she said. "They've built a new one down on the main level," she said, pointing to an enclosed glass room not far from the altar.

"So this isn't used at all?"

"Not normally, no. I'm sure with the crowd today, though, they might open it up for overflow." She looked around. "It holds maybe forty people."

Sam walked to the glass, her view of the congregation unimpeded. The main area was nearly full. At the front, she noticed several pews full of younger men similarly dressed in black.

"They're from the seminary," Marissa supplied, following her gaze.

"How many priests does Saint Mary's have?"

"Six that are here full time, not counting Monsignor Bernard. Well, five now that Father Michael is gone. I'm told the seminarians help celebrate daily Mass only. I'm not quite sure about all the rules they have about who can say a Mass and whatnot. Do you know?"

"I should know, I suppose," Sam said. "The fact is, my brother and I hardly communicate at all."

"Because you're gay?" Marissa asked quietly.

Sam shook her head. "He doesn't know. Neither do my parents."

"Really?"

Sam shrugged. "They live in Denver, he's in Brazil. I haven't seen my parents in several years and conversations on the phone are infrequent." She smiled. "Besides, it's a rather recent discovery."

"Tori's your first?"

Sam nodded. "Does that surprise you?"

"Somewhat, yes. But I take it you're very committed?"

"Very." Sam felt the flush on her face, but she continued, feeling at ease with the conversation. "I had no idea what being in love felt like until I met her. And now I can't possibly imagine my life without her in it." She met Marissa's gaze. "What about you?"

"Perpetually single," Marissa said. She pointed down below them. "Those are four of the priests. Looks like they're going to assist with Mass."

"With Monsignor Bernard?"

"No. Bishop Lewis is doing the service. I believe the monsignor will read the Liturgy."

"You seem very well versed in it all. You did your homework there too?"

Marissa laughed. "I spent nearly eighteen months working with the diocese in Boston. I know all the verbiage." She moved away from the glass and took a seat on one of the benches. "I'm curious. How far are you and Hunter willing to go on this sexual affair you're convinced Father Michael was having?"

"How far? You act as if we're intent on exposing him and nothing more." Sam too moved away from the glass. "We believe it *is* relevant to his murder. And frankly, I couldn't care less if he had a sex life or not. It's not like I would get some sort of perverse pleasure from exposing it."

"Yet if it was made public, you can imagine the damage the diocese would suffer, can't you?"

"A priest having consensual sex with an adult, even if it is another man, cannot be compared to the sex abuse scandal of years past, when most of that involved children and young boys. It's not the same thing."

"Of course it is. They're breaking their vows. Sex is taboo. For most parishioners, the idea that their priest is having a sexual relationship with another man—an ongoing relationship at that—is unthinkable. The sex abuse scandal, as sick as it was, was looked upon as a few misguided men who were just that—sick. But an affair, a conscious choice made by the priest to be involved sexually with another man, that just wouldn't be tolerated."

Sam scoffed. "And that's just crazy."

"But that's the world we live in." She spread her hands. "Especially here."

"So I take it you are aware of the affair?"

"In no way do I mean that." Marissa shook her head. "I wouldn't tell you if I did know about it, of course, but I don't. There hasn't been even a word mentioned about it. Monsignor Bernard appeared quite shocked that I would even broach the subject with him."

"Well, I'm sure you've read the report from the crime lab. He can't dispute that. Or have you not shared it with him?"

"No, I haven't. But just because there was DNA evidence of another man in his bed doesn't make it sexual. It could be completely innocent."

"Like he just loaned his bed to someone?"

"Exactly."

"Even though there are two other bedrooms in the rectory?"

Marissa smiled. "I didn't say it would be easy to convince someone it was innocent."

Sam turned again toward the glass when organ music sounded again, followed by the soft vocals of the choir. She assumed the service was about to begin. She scanned the crowd, not really surprised to see Lieutenant Malone sitting near the back with who she assumed was his wife. She'd only seen pictures. She said to Marissa, "Off the record, do you think he was having an affair?"

Marissa laughed. "No way would I answer this question if it was Hunter doing the asking. But you . . . you have a bit of trustworthiness about you. So yes, I think he was having an affair."

"Is it too bold of me to ask who with?"

"That, I couldn't even speculate a guess," she said. "Which is why I assume you're here. You want to see if someone is grieving a little more than usual?"

Sam nodded. "Or perhaps if someone is celebrating his death instead of grieving." She shrugged. "Juan Hidalgo was the killer, yes. The why of it is what we want to know."

"You don't think he acted alone?"

"You're not probing for your next news brief, are you?"

"I thought we were off the record," Marissa said easily.

Sam hesitated. Tori would kill her if she knew she was divulging this information. But for some reason, she trusted Marissa. She also knew they needed her as an ally. "We suspect that Juan was coerced in some way."

"And who do you think killed Juan?"

"There were no physical findings. Whoever killed him did so without leaving a trace."

"And without forced entry."

Sam raised an eyebrow. "Is there anything about these cases you *don't* know?"

"I must admit, I have been given free access to your police reports. Which is something I wasn't expecting. After the service, I'll be speaking to the media again. I promise I won't divulge anything you've told me." She gave Sam a sincere smile. "Despite what you all think, we really do want you to solve his murder. We just don't want the diocese dragged through the mud in the process."

"Can I ask you something? Again, off the record," Sam added.

"Ask away."

"Who hired you?"

Marissa averted her gaze, peering down to the congregation below. "I know you think this is all some big attempt at a cover-up, but it's not." She paused. "It is what it is. Much like a political campaign, I'm here to put a positive spin on the church—the murder, on Father Michael himself—anything to avoid even the tiniest mention of a possible sex scandal."

"But why is the police department—the mayor, even—so cooperative?"

"Amazing, but not even the local media has picked up on it. Father Michael and your mayor . . . they're brothers."

"Are you serious? But why would he want to keep silent about it?"

"Politics. Everything is politics, Samantha."

"I don't understand." Sam was no stranger to politics, but this truly baffled her.

"If it was discovered that Father Michael was involved in a homosexual relationship, and then murdered, the media coverage would not just be local, or even statewide. There would be national press. A Catholic priest, a very popular Catholic priest at that, leading a secret life, one that crossed over to the dark side, so to speak. It wouldn't just be a blurb in the paper."

"So he wants to keep it quiet out of embarrassment?"

"No. But as popular as Father Michael was, Gerald Stevens is equally as popular in the political arena. So popular, in fact, he plans to run for the U.S. Senate."

"Wait a minute. He plans to run for the Senate?" Sam moved away from the window and sat down next to Marissa. "Forgive my ignorance in all this, but how in the world does he plan to keep the existence of his brother a secret? For that matter, the murder?"

"It wouldn't be that difficult. Mayor Stevens's parents divorced when he was a child. His father got custody and his mother got sent to rehab. Drugs. That's something else you probably won't hear about. And why would you? It's not relevant to his politics. Besides, his father remarried and had two more kids, so there's a whole new family. That's what I learned from the mayor. My own research revealed that he was a troubled teen, to say the least. He's got a rather lengthy juvenile record."

"Father Michael?"

"No. Mayor Stevens. It was during that time that their mother resurfaced and got custody of Michael, in part because Gerald was so out of control. But if you're looking at a bio of Mayor Stevens, you get father, stepmother and two stepsisters. No mention of a brother."

Sam shook her head. "First of all, his juvenile records could not be made public. I'm wondering how you got access to them. Secondly, why are you researching the man who hired you?"

"I believe in being thorough. And yes, his juvenile records *are* sealed." She smirked. "And no, I can't tell you how I gained access to them. But it also piqued my curiosity—just as it has yours—as to why he didn't want anyone to know Father Michael was his brother."

"I still don't understand the necessity to keep that a secret."

"Voters are fickle. Are you going to vote for a man whose brother defied the Catholic Church, disregarded his vows and had an affair with another man? You're in the conservative South. That constitutes a scandal."

"Give me a break. Politicians are scandalous in themselves, and others have been voted into office with far worse skeletons than having a gay brother."

"A gay brother who was a Catholic priest. A priest involved in a love affair. A priest possibly murdered because of that love affair."

"That's still no reason to think voters would shun him because of that."

"But why take that chance? Stevens has no relationship with his mother, but he and Michael had become close in the last few years. To an outsider, it was simply a man and wife having the occasional dinner with a priest, which was how Stevens wanted it. At the time, he was far more worried about his mother's drug problem being exposed."

"So when his brother was found murdered—found naked—he panicked?"

Marissa smiled. "This *is* all off the record, right?"

"Of course." Then Sam smiled too. "Well, I don't keep things from Tori."

"I didn't imagine that you would." Marissa went back to the glass, watching the procession. "It's started," she stated. She turned back. "Mayor Stevens contacted Bishop Lewis, offered the police department's total cooperation and offered to run interference with the media."

"Which is where you come in."

"Exactly. Which is why he wants this case solved, closed and done away with."

Sam walked closer, standing shoulder to shoulder with Marissa Goddard, both of them looking out over the church. Sam spotted the mayor, sitting alongside the police chief, several rows from the front. At the altar, Monsignor Bernard stood solemnly to the side as another man—she assumed Bishop Lewis—raised both hands in front of him, palms skyward, his voice echoing through the speakers.

"In the name of the Father . . ."

CHAPTER TWELVE

"Damn, Kennedy, look at you," Sikes said after a long wolf whistle. "You should show your legs more often."

Sam laughed good-naturedly as Sikes and Ramirez ogled her in her short skirt and heels.

"You wore that to the funeral?"

"I did. It's navy. It's perfectly appropriate."

"I'm surprised Hunter let you out of the house."

"Speaking of Tori, where is she?"

"She went over to the crime lab. She and Mac were going over the list of names she wants to print."

Sam nodded, thinking how convenient it was, now that the crime lab and the medical examiner were housed in the new building not two blocks away. Last year, they were still across town.

"Well, I should go change," she said. "Tori was supposed to

bring my bag."

"Yeah. It's on your chair."

She pulled her chair away from her desk, finding the bag. She was on her way to the ladies' room when Lieutenant Malone came into the squad room. He too was still dressed in the suit he'd worn to the funeral. He seemed surprised to see her dressed similarly.

"Kennedy, you made it?"

"To the funeral? Yes."

"I never saw you."

"I was upstairs in the old cry room," she said. "With Marissa Goddard."

"Sleeping with the enemy, are you?" Sikes asked.

"Actually, she was quite friendly," Sam said. "Maybe because Tori wasn't around," she added with a smile. "They seem to rub each other the wrong way."

Malone nodded. "Well, I need to see you. You and Hunter both. Where is she?"

"She's just over at the lab," Tony said. "You want me to call her?"

"Yeah." He pointed at Sam. "Go change. You don't even look like yourself."

Sam chuckled. "Same to you, Lieutenant. At least take the tie off."

When he walked away, her smile faded. He wanted to see them. Not Sikes and Ramirez too. Just them. So that meant it had nothing to do with the case. That meant it was personal. She gripped the bag tighter, her gaze alternating between Sikes and Ramirez.

"What does he want to see you about?" John asked. "He looked serious."

"I have no idea," she murmured as she went toward the restroom. She'd really hoped she would have a chance to talk to Tori about what Marissa had said, about them having to split up. She wanted them to be prepared for whatever Malone had to tell them. So, as she slipped out of the skirt and into the navy pants she'd packed that morning, she called Tori's cell.

Tori answered on the second ring. "Hunter."

"It's me. Where are you?"

"Waiting on you."

Sam looked at the door and frowned. "Where?"

"I just got here. I'm chatting with the lieutenant. He said he wanted to talk to us."

Sam bit her lower lip as she stared at the ceiling. "Okay. I'll be there in a minute." She folded her phone, then tossed it back and forth between her hands, hating the feeling of impending doom that had her in its grips. It would be her, she knew. Tori was too valuable here. No way they would send her somewhere. But Sam, yeah. *You're expendable.* Back to Assault, probably. Or worse. They could ship her off to Narcotics.

She quickly tucked in her blouse, then grabbed the suit jacket she'd worn to the funeral, wishing Marissa Goddard had never told her what she'd overheard. She stopped in mid-stride when she saw Tori, looking so relaxed as she spoke with Malone. She had no idea what was coming.

He said, "Kennedy, come in. Close the door."

Sam nodded as she shut the door. She stood there for a moment, her eyes on Malone. He looked as nervous as she felt.

"Sit down, Sam," he said.

"So, what's this big news, Lieutenant?" Tori asked impatiently. "We've got people to print. Mac's already sending his guys over there."

Malone nodded. "Yeah. Well, as you know, I met with the captain yesterday afternoon. Seems CIU has made a personnel request."

Tori frowned. "What are you talking about?"

"They're looking to promote someone. A detective," he said, looking at Sam, then Tori.

Tori's eyes widened. "What the hell?" She pointed at herself. "Me? You've got to be kidding."

"Yeah, Hunter, I'd have to be kidding," he said with a laugh. "I think you're a little too volatile for CIU. Besides, insubordinate is not one of the qualities they're looking for." He paused as he took a sip of his coffee. "They want Kennedy."

Tori looked at her and Sam saw the shock in Tori's eyes. "They want to split us up," Tori stated. She looked back at Malone. "Why?"

"You know why, Hunter. Hell, everyone knows why. Did you think they were going to let you keep working together indefinitely?"

Feeling less than confident, Sam stood. "But, Lieutenant, we're a good team. And I'm not interested in CIU. They'll have me stuck at a desk fielding phone calls and shuffling papers. I want to stay here."

"Samantha, I'm sorry, but it's not really a choice. And I think you'll like the assignment. You know Detective Travis, of course. He's made lieutenant. He'll be getting his own team. He personally requested you."

"But—"

"It's a good opportunity, Kennedy." He looked at Tori. "It's for the best. Travis will treat her good. If she's going to move up, CIU is where she needs to be, not stuck here in Homicide. You know that."

Tori stood too, both hands clasping her head, her fingers threading over and over again through her hair. "Wow," she murmured. "CIU."

Sam let out a deep breath, not knowing what to say to Tori. The life they had, the partnership they had here at work—it was comfortable. They were a team. And she knew Tori was terrified. "What are we going to do?" she asked quietly.

"Doesn't look like we have a choice." Tori stared at Malone. "Done deal?"

"Afraid so."

"And there's nothing you can do? I mean, Stan, we're good together. Hell, you know me and partners."

"I know you're good together. And believe me, I do know you and partners. But you're in a relationship," he said. "And as much as we were willing to let that fly here, the brass is not." He shuffled through papers on his desk, finding the orders he had been given. He handed it to Sam. "You've got the weekend off. On Monday, you report to Travis at CIU. Simple as that."

"Monday? But what about our case?" Sam asked.

"Our case consists mainly of Hidalgo now." He took another sip of his coffee, no doubt cold by now, Sam thought. "After the final M.E.'s report, they want Special Victims involved."

Tori spun around. "What the hell? Jackson said no sexual trauma. There wasn't indication of assault. You read the report."

"I know that, Hunter. But it wasn't what the chief wanted to hear."

Sam watched Tori, saw the disbelief on her face, no doubt matching her own.

"They're making Jackson alter his report? Are you *kidding* me?"

"No. They haven't stooped that far yet. But if they involve Special Victims, it will appear to the public as if he was assaulted, whether it was the truth or not."

"Unbelievable. So they're just taking over our case?"

He shook his head. "Not exactly. They're sending over one of their detectives. They'll work with us on the case. Goddard will mention it in her next news briefing on Monday. From what I gathered, they want it done this week. Father Michael was assaulted during his murder. Hidalgo is the murderer. Case closed."

"This is just fucking unbelievable," Tori said, her voice rising. "It's as if our own department is doing a cover-up, not the church. And here comes Special Victims. They'll wrap this case up in a week and make us look as incompetent as I feel right now."

Sam hesitated, Marissa's words still echoing in her brain. But she'd promised her their conversation was off the record so she said nothing. She would discuss it with Tori later.

"Look, there's nothing I can do about it, Hunter. Now, we're still going to match the prints. It's still technically our case. And we don't know who killed Hidalgo. We're not just sweeping that one under the rug, you know."

"Not yet. But if our prints turn up something, no doubt that'll turn into a cold case quick."

Malone sighed. "Drop it, Hunter." He looked at Sam. "Did you get anything at the funeral? I didn't notice anything out of the ordinary."

"Actually, I spent most of the time talking with Marissa," she said with a glance at Tori. "We had an out-of-the-way spot to watch."

Tori stared at her. "Out-of-the-way?"

"They used to have the cry room upstairs," she said. "It's no longer used."

Tori smirked. "I see. And what did the devious Ms. Goddard have to say?"

Sam shrugged. "Nothing pertinent, really. She assumed I wanted to observe, so she took me someplace where I could monitor it in secrecy." She looked back at Tori. "She was . . . friendly."

Malone watched the staredown between them, finally clearing his throat before speaking. "Well, we won't have much more to go on until the crime lab gets those prints. Hunter, why don't we pick it up again on Monday? Give the lab time to do their thing." He said to Sam, "Take a long weekend. I know this change is a shock to you both. And we're going to all miss you being around here, Kennedy."

Sam nodded, looking out his windows into the squad room.

"Do they know?"

"No. I was just informed late yesterday. I haven't told anyone."

She nodded again. She'd miss it here as well, and not just because of Tori. Sikes had become a good friend to them, Tony too. And Malone, for all his gruffness, was like a father to them. No matter what, he stood by them, had stood by Tori for all those years. So she reached across his desk and took his hand, squeezing hard. "Thank you for all you've done, Lieutenant. For me." She glanced at Tori. "For us."

"Hell, Kennedy, it's not like we won't see you around, right?"

She smiled. "Of course."

He stood, then surprised her by pulling her into a hug. "You've been good for us, Samantha," he said. "I wish you nothing but the best."

"Thanks, Lieutenant. That means a great deal to me." She pulled away, telling herself she wouldn't choke up. "I think we might take you up on that offer of a long weekend." She turned to Tori. "Okay?"

Grim-faced, Tori nodded. "Sure. Whatever you want. But you better let the guys know."

She left without another word, and Sam turned to Malone. "She's not going to take this well."

"Oh, I don't know. She didn't throw a chair or anything."

Sam paused at the door. "Do you already have someone in mind for her new partner, Lieutenant?"

"Actually, you're not the only one leaving the squad, Samantha. Ramirez got tabbed to be a part of a taskforce. Little Mexico."

"Drugs?"

"Yeah. The taskforce won't report to Narcotics though. They'll report straight to CIU." He looked past her out the window. "He doesn't know it yet."

"And Sikes?"

Malone chuckled. "Never thought I'd live to see this day, but he and Hunter are going to be partners." He met her eyes. "You think it'll work out?"

She imagined Sikes and Tori as partners and nodded. "I don't think you could find anyone better. They get along fine now, Lieutenant. I think they'll be great together."

"Well, I don't know about great." He held the door open for her. "You better go find Hunter."

"Tori," Sam called as she pushed the door to the ladies' room open. Tori was at the sink, staring into the mirror, her face still wet where she'd splashed it. Sam studied Tori's eyes in the reflection of the glass. Worried eyes. "You okay?"

Tori grabbed a couple of paper towels and patted her face dry, then sighed. "Yeah, I'm okay," she finally said. "You?"

Sam moved closer, pausing to rest one hip against the sink. She folded her arms, watching Tori. "I'm not sure. It's a bit of a shock."

"Yeah. Yeah, it is." Tori turned. "But like he said, it's a good opportunity for you. And you know, Travis, he's a good man. He's honest. He'll do right by you."

Sam nodded but didn't say anything for a moment. She was a little troubled by what she saw in Tori's eyes. Doubt. Insecurity. Things she hadn't seen in a very long time. She had an idea. "You know, I was thinking. It's supposed to be a nice weekend, not too cold. Maybe we could head out to the boat, spend the weekend."

"Like now?" Tori asked, her eyes brightening just a little.

"Yeah. I mean, I know you wanted to clean out your apartment this weekend, but maybe that could wait."

Tori turned away. "Well, I may just keep it. You know, never know when I might need it."

Sam frowned. "Need it? Why in the world would you need it?" She shoved off the sink and moved beside Tori. "You tired of living with me already?" she asked lightly.

"No, Sam. Nothing like that." Tori took a step away, nervously glancing around the room. "But you know, things are going to change, be different."

Sam stared at her. "Change? You mean, you think I'll get tired of living with you?"

Tori shrugged. "You might."

Sam wondered what had brought on this line of thinking. "Then you obviously have no idea how much I love you." She came closer, their bodies nearly touching. "Whether we work together or not, Tori, that won't change." Resting her hand at Tori's waist, she felt her tremble at her touch, and she moved closer. "Let's go to the boat," she whispered. "We need to be alone. No interruptions." She slid her hand down to Tori's hip. "Can we?"

Tori closed her eyes for a moment, the expression on her face one of uncertainty. Finally, she let out her breath and opened her eyes, nodding.

"Good." Sam leaned closer, gently brushing her lips against Tori's. "Because I want to make love to you."

CHAPTER THIRTEEN

"It's going to be a beautiful night," Sam said as she pulled their chairs out on the deck after Tori had docked in their favorite cove. "We haven't sat out and watched the moon in forever."

"Kinda hard in the city," Tori said.

"Which is why we need to come to the lake more often." She took the wineglass Tori handed her. "Thanks."

Tori sat down beside her, and they watched the night sky in silence, the moon already rising over the trees on this short January evening. Really, it was the time of year Tori hated. No green, no vibrancy. No peepers, no crickets, no sound. Just the quiet splashing of the water as the boat bobbed gently on the surface.

Tori pulled her gaze from the moon, watching Sam. Sam finally turned her head, meeting her eyes. "You going to tell me what you learned today?"

"What makes you think I learned something?"

"Because you made a point to tell Malone you didn't."

Sam nodded. "I see." She took a sip of wine, hesitating. "You want to talk about Marissa first, or you want to talk about me leaving?"

Tori turned back to the moon, afraid. "I'm not sure I ever want to talk about you leaving," she said. "It's a little frightening, to be honest."

Sam entwined her fingers with Tori's. "Nothing to be frightened about. I promise." She squeezed Tori's hand. "You trust me, don't you?"

Tori nodded. "Yes."

"Okay." She squeezed her hand again before releasing it. "We'll talk about me leaving tonight. In bed," she added.

Tori stared at the moon, hating that she felt insecure, hating that she was afraid their life was about to change. And it was a life she now knew she couldn't live without, a life where she felt happy, complete, content—all those things she never thought she deserved before.

"Sam?"

"Hmm?"

Tori hesitated for only a moment. "I love you."

She watched as Sam took a sharp breath. Sam always did. Three little words. But still, they were three words she rarely said. She still couldn't forget her childhood, was still afraid she would be left behind, left alone. And on those occasions when something touched her, when something made her utter those words—like tonight—she knew Sam felt the true meaning of them. Not just three words that were spoken so casually by most, three words tossed about without thought. When she spoke them, they came from her heart. Totally.

She felt Sam reach between them again, felt Sam slide her hand across her arm to her hand, their fingers joining. They said

90

nothing, just sat quietly holding hands. Finally, she relaxed. "Now, are you ready to tell me what Marissa said?"

Sam laughed. "Time to get back to business?" She held out her wineglass. "Fill me up, please."

"Are you enjoying keeping me in the dark?" Tori said as she topped off the wineglass. "And just how friendly did Ms. Goddard get?"

Sam laughed again. "Oh, my God, you're not jealous, are you?"

"Of course not. It's just that I would never consider her friendly, that's all."

"Actually, she was quite nice and, surprisingly, quite forthcoming."

"Oh, yeah?"

"We talked, Tori." Sam looked at her. "We talked . . . off the record."

"What does that mean?"

"That means we can't tell anyone."

"Tell anyone? What the hell did she say?"

Sam took Tori's hand again. "I'm serious, Tori. What she told me was off the record."

Their eyes held in the dim light, Tori realizing that Sam was serious. "Okay, fine. Off the record."

"Okay, good. Then get this. The church didn't bring Marissa in. *We* did," she said.

"What the hell?"

"At the request of the mayor."

"Buy why?"

"Because Mayor Stevens and Father Michael were brothers."

"*What?*"

"And the sex scandal they're trying to prevent has nothing to do with protecting the church and everything to do with Stevens's political future."

Tori stood and walked to the railing, looking out over the

dark lake, seeing nothing. *Goddamn politics.* "Unbelievable." She turned back around. "What political future?" she asked. "Is he planning on running for governor or something?"

"U.S. Senate," Sam said.

Tori frowned. "What the hell does that have to do with his brother?"

"Marissa didn't say directly, but I assumed that Stevens knew his brother was having an affair. So when he was found naked, Stevens figured it would come out."

"So, short of telling us and the crime lab to alter evidence, he ties our hands with the media."

"Exactly."

"Isn't that going a bit far? We all know cover-ups eventually come out. And for what? I still don't see how this affects his political career."

"I don't either, but what do we know about politics?"

"And why the hell did she share this with you?"

"Because, Tori, she really does want to help with the case."

"Oh, Sam, come on. Surely you're not that naïve? She doesn't *care* about this case. She's here to make this case go away."

Sam grabbed her hand and pulled her back into her chair. "I just think she can be an ally, Tori, if you let her. There was just something about her demeanor today. I mean, she didn't have to tell me any of this. I think there's a part of her that really hates what she's doing."

"We're not going to be allies, Sam. I don't even like the woman."

"Yes, you've made that obvious."

"Well, I don't like cover-ups. And she's a part of it."

Sam smiled gently. "We're all a part of it, sweetheart. Whether we want to be or not."

Tori sighed. "Yeah. We are, aren't we." She leaned back, attempting a smile. "But you're about out of this mess, aren't you?" She took a deep breath, then met Sam's eyes. She saw Sam searching, wondering what she saw there, wondering if she could see the fear, the uncertainty.

"You want to talk about it now?"

Tori shrugged. "I don't do real well with change, I guess."

"Tori, our life together, what we have outside of this job, that's so precious to me, I wouldn't do anything to change that." She squeezed her hand. "Our days will be different, yes. But our *life*, that won't change."

Tori watched her, realizing for the first time that Sam was taking this whole thing pretty calmly. In fact, she'd hardly seemed surprised when Malone told them. "How long have you known?"

Sam looked away, but not before Tori saw the embarrassment on her face. *Busted.*

"Marissa?"

Sam nodded. "She told me at the funeral that she'd heard they were going to reassign one of us. When I got back and Malone said he wanted to see us, I knew then what it was about." She handed her wineglass to Tori when she held out the bottle. "That's why I called you, but you were already in Malone's office. I was going to warn you."

"So, you're really okay with this?"

"I don't know, Tori. I mean, it's a good opportunity, sure. But I love working with you. I love the team we have in our whole department." She paused. "More than that, I'm going to lose that security I have."

"What do you mean?"

She faced Tori. "I know that with you, I'll always be safe. I know you would never let anything happen to me," she said quietly. "I trust you with my life."

And that's what Tori was really afraid of. If something were to happen, she wouldn't be there to protect Sam. She wouldn't be there to look after her. But she pushed those fears away, thinking them silly. Sam was plenty capable of looking after herself.

"Maybe it's me losing the security," Tori said. "Who's going to keep me out of trouble?"

Sam laughed. "You don't think Sikes can handle you?"

Tori frowned. "Sikes?" She saw Sam bite her lower lip. *Ah, a secret.* But she waited, knowing Sam wouldn't keep it from her.

"Malone told me that Tony is being reassigned too. They're creating a taskforce to work Little Mexico."

"Damn, they're splitting up the whole team, huh?"

"Ramirez is bilingual. It makes sense."

"And he doesn't know yet?"

"No. Malone told me on our way out today. I don't know if that's immediate or what."

"Unbelievable," Tori murmured. "It's fucking unbelievable."

Sam wrapped her fingers around Tori's arm, squeezing softly. "It's going to be okay, Tori. At least you and Sikes . . . well, you guys get along fine now. At least they're not bringing in someone totally new, you know."

"No. We just get to play with Special Victims for a while, that's all."

Sam squeezed her arm again, then stood up. "You know what? I've had enough talking for the night." She took Tori's wineglass and tugged on her arm. "Come on."

Tori smiled. "Come on?"

"Yeah. Come." She raised both eyebrows teasingly. "I'm ready to get you naked."

Tori laughed. "Come?"

Sam bent down, her mouth covering Tori's, wiping the smile from her face. "You want to?" she whispered seductively.

CHAPTER FOURTEEN

"Who the hell is that?" Sikes whispered.

Tori looked up. A tall woman strode confidently into the squad room, her gaze moving over them quickly before she stopped at Malone's door. She nodded briefly in their direction.

"Cute," Sikes said.

"You think?"

She was tall, although not as tall as Tori. Her light brown hair barely covered the collar of her blouse, and Tori watched as the woman brushed her bangs to the side, then knocked on Malone's door.

"Special Victims?" Sikes asked.

"I imagine." It was barely ten on Monday morning, and already the fun was beginning. She flicked her gaze to Sam's empty chair, already missing her being with them.

"Detective O'Connor?"

"Casey, please," she said as she shook hands with Malone. "Nice to finally meet you."

"Same here." He looked out his window, then back at O'Connor. "Have a seat. Let me bring in Hunter and Sikes. No sense in going over everything twice."

He stepped outside his office, and she watched him, watched the two detectives he spoke with. They weren't happy with her appearance here, she could tell that. And she wasn't exactly thrilled to be here, either. She'd been on the other end before, in the middle of an investigation when it was suddenly turned over to Homicide after it was determined no sexual crime had been committed. Although this was the only time she could remember Homicide giving up a case to Special Victims. Especially a high-profile case such as this.

"Detective Casey O'Connor, this is Tori Hunter and John Sikes. They've been the lead on this case. I believe you'll find their reports very thorough." He added, "Detective O'Connor is from Special Victims."

She stood quickly, offering her hand to both Hunter and Sikes. Hunter met her eyes unflinchingly, although she didn't try to hide the distrust there. Sikes gave her a charming smile and a subtle wink. She returned the smile, minus the wink.

"I've already read your reports. Very meticulous on details." She sat down again. "My captain has gone over my role here, Lieutenant. I'm not exactly thrilled with it," she said. "As I'm sure neither are your detectives," she added with a glance at Hunter. She was surprised to see a quick glimpse of understanding there.

"Well, then, perhaps you know more than we do," Malone admitted. "Hunter, Sikes, sit down. Let's talk this out."

"The M.E.'s report didn't indicate there was any sexual

assault," Casey said. "My captain . . . well, he said I needed to find some." She looked at Hunter. "Your notes say you think he was involved in a consensual sexual relationship."

"Right," Tori replied. "Based on the DNA evidence found in the bed, as well as evidence of sexual activity, but no evidence of trauma."

"Then why the hell am I here?"

"To prove it was Juan Hidalgo who killed him, and to prove that he was assaulted," Tori said.

Casey looked around the room, meeting the eyes of each of them, surprised at the near contempt they held. But it wasn't aimed at her. It was aimed at the system.

"I think it'd have just been easier to have Jackson lie in his report, if they're trying to fix the case," she said.

"You've heard about the consultant? Goddard?" Tori asked.

"Yeah. I hear she's got balls," she said with a smile.

"Wouldn't doubt it," Tori murmured. "But she's pushing the sexual assault. So far, it's been mentioned in nearly every news briefing. It's only logical they bring in Special Victims."

Casey leaned forward. "You think Hidalgo did it?"

"Strangled him? Yes. No doubt."

She nodded. "So why not just end the case now? Hidalgo is the murderer. End of story."

"Because it's not the end of the goddamn story. It's only the beginning. There is no motive. And the fact that Hidalgo was killed within hours indicates there's a third party." Tori looked at Sikes. "Did you and Tony have any luck trying to locate that guy from the bar?"

"No. Carlos split town. We hung out at the bar Saturday night," he said. "I don't mind saying, I was plenty scared. They made me for a cop right off."

Tori laughed. "Showed up as your usual *GQ* self, huh?"

"But Tony, man, he fit right in. He'll do good with this new taskforce."

"Excuse me, but are you talking about the guy who gave Hidalgo a ride from the bar?" Casey asked. "This is the bar where Hidalgo supposedly said *God* told him to kill?"

"The third party. But I doubt seriously it was God," Sikes said with a grin.

She nodded. "Okay. Well, I've read your files, read your notes. I think before I make my own assumptions, I'd like to interview the housekeeper again. She's the one who found him, right?"

"Yeah. And we've talked to her twice. Alice Hagen. She hasn't changed her story."

Casey stood. "Then let's don't ask her questions. Let's tell her what we know." She looked at Malone. "I don't guess you want me going solo."

"Take Hunter. She's familiar with the housekeeper."

"Good. Thanks." She turned to Tori. "I didn't have breakfast. Mind if we stop for an early lunch?"

"I know a great drive-thru. You can eat in the car."

"Yeah. Didn't take you for the sit-down type." She reached across the desk and shook Malone's hand. "I'll stay out of your hair, promise." She turned to Sikes. "Nice to meet you, John."

He nodded. "Let me know if I can help with anything."

"Absolutely." She glanced at Tori as she pulled out her cell and headed to the door. "I just have a quick call to make," she said as she walked out of the office.

"Well, what do you think?" Malone asked as soon as O'Connor was gone.

"I think there are too many damn lesbians on the force," Tori said.

Malone shook his head. "About the case, Hunter. The case."

She shrugged. "Well, at least she's not just ignoring the evidence. But her captain has pretty much given her the order, so yeah, I guess it'll be wrapped up this week."

"I know you don't like this, Hunter. But at least it's not like we're letting a killer go. We all know Hidalgo did it."

"So because he killed a priest, we shouldn't be concerned with finding out who killed him?" She glared at him, her anger growing. "Because that's just crap."

"I didn't say that. But if they want to close the case on Father Michael, if they want to pretend he was assaulted, then fine. Should we really care? Does it matter that he may have been involved with someone?"

"It's a dangerous precedent to set by withholding the facts." She paused. "Or worse, ignoring them."

Malone looked at Sikes and raised his eyebrows questioningly.

"I have to agree with Hunter. We may know who killed Father Michael, but we're nowhere near the truth of it all."

Malone smiled. "Damn."

"What?"

"You two agreeing. You two getting along." He laughed. "Hell, you two partners. Whoever would have thought it?"

CHAPTER FIFTEEN

Tori tapped her fingers impatiently on the steering wheel of the Explorer as they waited at the drive-thru for O'Connor's burger. She looked at her watch yet again, then sighed. They'd been in line nearly ten minutes.

"So, I hear you and your old partner, Kennedy, are an item," Casey said.

Tori turned her head. "You hear? From who?"

Casey shrugged. "When I found out I'd be working this case, I did a little checking. No offense, but you have a hell of a reputation, Hunter."

"And not all good?" Tori asked dryly. "I'm just shocked."

"So it's true? That's why she got transferred?"

"It's true," Tori said, turning as the window opened and a young girl held a bag out.

"Need ketchup?" the girl asked.

"No," Tori said quickly, grabbing the bag.

"Yeah, ketchup. Got fries in there, you know."

Tori looked back at the girl. "Yes, ketchup." She handed Casey the bag. "Do you eat like this every day?"

"What do you mean?" she asked as she shoved a french fry into her mouth, minus the ketchup.

Tori looked over her slender figure and shook her head. "Nothing." She held out her hand for the ketchup packets, tossing them at Casey as she drove away.

"Are you always in such a hurry?" Casey asked, holding on to the dash as Tori pulled out into traffic.

Tori ignored her as she changed lanes, albeit somewhat slower. She glanced at the other woman in disbelief as Casey took a big bite of her burger. "So, let's talk about it," she said. "No captain around, no lieutenant. Just us."

"Kinda hard to do when eating," Casey mumbled, her mouth full.

"Fine. I'll talk. We think Mrs. Hagen knows who Father Michael was having an affair with. In fact, we're positive she knows. We also think, obviously, that one of the thirteen prints found in the rectory belongs to whoever the affair was with."

Casey put her burger down and grabbed two fries, eating them before speaking. "Your notes said you thought the housekeeper was protecting Father Michael," she said.

"Yeah. And she would. She adored the man."

Casey dipped another fry into ketchup. "But what if she's not protecting Father Michael at all? What if she's protecting his lover?"

Tori frowned, staring straight ahead. The thought had never even crossed her mind. They'd been so sure she was protecting Father Michael, they hadn't even considered she also knew the lover.

"Good, O'Connor. We were focusing totally on Father Michael."

Casey grinned. "That's because you work in Homicide and you're used to focusing on the dead."

"Wait a minute? You think maybe it's another priest?"

"Could be. Could be that's why the church doesn't want it to get out."

Tori bit her lip. Sam would kill her. But it didn't matter. She couldn't let it go. "What I'm about to tell you is completely off the record and not to go any further." She looked at O'Connor. "Agreed?"

"Do we know each other well enough for this?"

"No. But it doesn't look like we're going to have a whole lot of time to learn to trust." Tori flipped on her blinker and turned on Milam.

She nodded. "Okay. Agreed."

"I have learned from a very good source that the church is not involved in this. Not willingly, anyway."

"What do you mean?"

"All of this cover-up bullshit is coming directly from the mayor's office."

"Oh, come on, Hunter." Casey shoved two fries into her mouth. "The mayor's not going to order a cover-up of a murder. Besides, the chief would never go for it. If it ever got out, it'd be career suicide."

"Look, I don't know you from Adam, but I don't have a whole lot of choice but to trust you. Because I don't want to close this case prematurely. There's something going on. There are too many higher-ups involved." Tori stole a glance at her. "The reason the mayor ordered the cover-up is because Father Michael was his brother."

"Are you fucking with me?"

"No, I'm not fucking with you," Tori hissed. "I'm goddamn serious."

"But why would he try to hide the fact that the priest was his brother?"

"I don't know. Hell, what do we know about politics?"

"How do you know this?"

Tori paused. "I can't say."

"You can't say? Well, goddamn, Hunter, how the hell are we supposed to follow up on it if you won't say who told you?"

"We're not going to follow up on it. I told you, it's off the record." She glanced at her again. "But at least we know why he's involved. He's got bigger political aspirations than just mayor."

"So this consultant, she's not really here because of the church?"

"Right. She was hired by the mayor."

"Which is how I got my dinner date," Casey murmured.

"What? What dinner date?"

"My captain said I had a dinner date tonight with Marissa Goddard. Said the chief set it up. She wants to meet with me and go over things, he said."

"Oh, sure she does. Just like she met with us to 'go over things.'" Tori turned and slowed. "The housekeeper lives just down the block."

Casey tossed the rest of her burger into the bag, along with a handful of fries that were smothered in ketchup. "Got a napkin in here, Hunter?"

"In the console there," she said. "And Mrs. Hagen isn't real fond of me. Sam usually did the talking."

"Sam? Your partner?"

Tori parked along the curb. "Kennedy, yeah, my partner." Without waiting for O'Connor, she hopped out and started toward the house.

Casey slammed her door, hurrying to catch up with her as she walked up the sidewalk. "So, how did that work out?"

Tori stopped. "What?"

"Working with your lover?"

"Obviously not too well. They split us up."

"No, I mean, for you. Was it weird living together *and* working together?"

"No, it wasn't weird, and why all the questions?"

Casey shrugged. "Just curious. I mean, I've known partners who've had an affair. Nothing long-lasting, mind you, but sex. And when it was over with, it screwed up their partnership. With you, you'd think working together would screw up your sex life."

Tori held up her hand. "Can we stop with the questions, please? It's irrelevant anyway. We don't work together any longer."

"All right, Hunter. And it's not like I'll be needing advice from you on the subject. My partner back at SV is a very happily married man."

Tori sighed. Couldn't be paired up with someone who didn't talk, could she? Jeez, the woman was a chatterbox. She reached out to push the doorbell, then stopped. "Are you done chatting? You ready for me to get Mrs. Hagen now?"

"Yeah, sure, Hunter. Go ahead. But, you know, maybe you should let me do the talking."

"Sure, O'Connor. Try sweet-talking her. Maybe it'll work for you." Tori pushed the doorbell and held it, then let up and pushed it again. She saw movement through the glass and heard the locks being turned. The door opened slowly and Mrs. Hagen peeked through the crack. Tori saw the dismay in her eyes.

"You again? What do you want this time?"

Casey stepped forward. "Actually, it's me, Mrs. Hagen. Detective Hunter was just kind enough to drive me over. I'm Detective O'Connor, from Special Victims, ma'am. May we come in?"

"I don't have anything else to say. I already told her that."

"I understand. And we don't really have many questions, Mrs. Hagen. I just wanted to fill you in, let you know what's going on."

The door opened a little wider. "Fill me in about what?"

Casey looked around. "You want to talk out here?" She

leaned closer. "Neighbors and all. Perhaps we should come inside."

Mrs. Hagen hesitated, looking across the street to the neighbor's house, then nodded. "Very well." She held the door open. "Come in."

Casey looked at Tori, then offered for her to go first. Tori rolled her eyes and stepped back.

"Fine. Be the bigger dyke," Casey murmured.

Tori managed to smother her laugh before following them inside. It was quiet this time, no noise from the TV drifting through the house. But something smelled delicious. Chicken soup? "How's your husband, Mrs. Hagen?" Tori asked as they went into the kitchen.

"He's not feeling well today. He's resting." She moved to the stove and lifted the lid on a pot, stirring slowly. "He'll be wanting his lunch soon."

"Well, we won't take up much of your time," Casey said. Standing by the small table, she pulled out a chair, spinning it around to face the stove and sat down, casually crossing her legs and resting one ankle on her knee. "I said earlier that I was from Special Victims. Do you know what that is, Mrs. Hagen?" When the older woman continued to silently stir the pot, she continued. "We investigate sexual crimes, Mrs. Hagen. Rape, sexual assault, murder caused by a sexual attack. Things like that." She glanced at Tori, who was watching Mrs. Hagen. "Just thought you'd like to know that we're going to close the case on Father Michael. Juan Hidalgo killed him. You knew Juan, right?" When she still didn't answer, Casey stood up and approached her. "Mrs. Hagen? Didn't you know Juan?"

She finally turned away from the stove. "Yes, I knew Juan. He'd worked there for several years."

"Bet it was a surprise then, right?"

"Of course. Juan was always so cordial, so polite. No one would have suspected he would be capable of murder."

105

Casey smiled. "Oh, murder, right. But I'm talking about the affair he was having with Father Michael."

"*What*?" Mrs. Hagen gasped.

"Yeah. We couldn't believe it either. But apparently they'd been having this big love affair for a while. It'll be on the news later in the week, as soon as we close the case."

"No." She shook her head. "No. They weren't . . . they weren't having an *affair*," she whispered.

"They had to have been, Mrs. Hagen. The medical examiner says he'd had sex," she said matter-of-factly. "The way we figure it, the affair went sour, or they got into a lovers' quarrel or something. Juan snapped and strangled him." She paused. "Just like that, Mrs. Hagen. Just goes to show, you never know, right?"

"No. No, they weren't."

"Mrs. Hagen, there's no need to protect him any longer. We know you knew. I mean, you're the housekeeper. You know everything that goes on in the house, right?" She turned and pushed the chair back under the table. "Detective Hunter here tells me she asked you who he was having an affair with. We understand why you wouldn't say anything, Mrs. Hagen. I mean, Juan Hidalgo, who would have thought? But it's all over now."

"It's going to be on the news?"

"Yeah. I feel bad for Father Michael. I mean, he didn't want anyone to know, obviously. Now it'll be all over TV." She came closer. "But Juan? He just didn't seem his type, you know?"

She shook her head. "It wasn't Juan. It was never Juan."

"Mrs. Hagen, you told me you didn't know of an affair," Tori reminded her. "You said Father Michael wasn't involved with anyone. Are you trying to protect him or Juan?"

Just then an elderly man, humped over a walker with oxygen tubes attached to his nose, shuffled into the kitchen. "Alice? Who are these people?"

"They're just leaving." She looked at them quickly, then went to her husband. "Come. It's time for lunch." Mrs. Hagen helped him to a chair, which Casey held out for him, then motioned for them to follow her out. "He has his doctor's appointment tomorrow," she said. "My daughter Kathleen always takes him." She glanced over her shoulder, back down the hallway. "Come by in the morning," she said quietly. "About ten."

"Mrs. Hagen?" Tori said.

She reached in the pocket of her housedress, her fingers moving nervously, and Tori knew she was fingering the rosary beads she always kept with her.

"Tomorrow. I must get back to him now."

She closed the door as they stood there, and Tori heard the distinct click of the deadbolt as she locked the door.

Casey grinned. "See? We got an invitation for coffee tomorrow. And if we're lucky, she'll bake banana bread or something."

Tori raised an eyebrow. "If we're lucky, she'll give up a name." She headed back to her Explorer, feeling like maybe they were going to get a break. Finally. She stopped at the curb. "Good work, by the way."

"Thanks, Hunter. I figured if she liked Father Michael as much as you all said she did, she wouldn't want his name soiled by the likes of Juan Hidalgo. You know, say you and I were good friends and I knew you were having an affair with Samantha Kennedy—who I hear is hot, by the way—and someone else is accusing you of having a fling with, say, Teresa Fillmore over in Central."

Tori laughed. In her mid-fifties, Teresa Fillmore was, as someone once called her, a dyke's dyke.

"Now, see, I wouldn't want people thinking you had bad taste. So I'd confess that no, it wasn't old, ugly Teresa you were having an affair with, but that cute, young Detective Kennedy." Casey opened the passenger door, pausing. "And I'd confess even if I knew it would get you into all sorts of trouble because being with Teresa Fillmore would just be gross."

"So you're going on the assumption that Alice Hagen is

simply appalled that we're closing this case, leaving everyone believing that Father Michael and Juan—his killer—were lovers. Is that right? So now she's just going to tell us the truth?"

"She's going to tell us the truth, yes, and I believe she's wrestling with it because it's another priest. Hell, it could even be someone from the seminary. Maybe that's why she's hesitant. I mean, Father Michael was what? Early forties? In her eyes, maybe she's trying to protect one of the young men there."

Tori made a U-turn in front of the Hagens' house, stopping at the end of the street before turning on Nichols Avenue. "If we get a name, our next step is to try to interview him. And good luck getting that out of Marissa Goddard."

"What's she like, anyway?"

"Obnoxious. Arrogant." She paused. "Cocky."

Casey laughed. "Damn, Hunter, you just described yourself."

Tori frowned. "What the hell are you talking about?"

"I also heard a straight woman say you were sexy."

Tori felt the flush creep over her face, which grew even warmer when O'Connor noticed.

"But anyone who blushes like that can't be cocky, right?" Casey teased.

"I don't think I like you," Tori murmured.

"Oh, hell, Hunter, everyone likes me. Now, about Goddard, really, what's she like? Is she cute?"

"Cute? Why the hell do you want to know if she's cute?"

"Because any woman who's called arrogant, obnoxious and cocky has *got* to be gay." Casey reached across the console and lightly punched Tori's arm. "So? Cute? Yes?"

Tori shook her head. Cute was the last thing on her mind when it came to Marissa Goddard. "No."

"No? Damn. And I've got a dinner date with her."

"Are you meeting somewhere?"

"No. Hell, she's picking me up." Casey stared at Tori. "How old is she? I mean, she's probably old, right?" She paused. "I should have never agreed to let her pick me up."

Tori chuckled, picturing the young, smartly dressed woman. "Yeah, she's old. In fact, she reminds me a little of Teresa Fillmore without the bleached hair."

Casey's eyes widened. "Are you serious? Okay, so tell me she's straight, she's got a husband back home, kids."

"Nope. She's gay." Of that, she was certain.

Casey scowled. "I hate you."

CHAPTER SIXTEEN

That night, Tori walked into their apartment and tossed her keys on the bar, hating the quiet, hating the darkness. In the kitchen, she opened the fridge, the light bouncing shadows across the room as she surveyed the contents without interest. Last night's dinner—leftover chicken spaghetti—was ready for the microwave, but she reached around it and grabbed a bottle of beer, easily twisting the cap off and flipping it into the trash.

Now nearly February, the days were getting a bit longer, and she went out onto the tiny deck, missing the last rays of sunshine but sitting down on a patio chair anyway. She hadn't talked to Sam all day and had no idea when she'd be home.

And she hated it—the empty house. It brought back . . . well, it brought back memories of her life before Sam, before she had a reason to come home. And it also made her realize how much her life had changed in the last year or so. She was no longer the arrogant, obnoxious bitch no one wanted to work with. No longer the first to arrive and the last to leave. No, now she had a life, had someone to share it with, someone to love, someone to *be* with. And God only knew why, but she also had someone who loved her.

So she pushed that tiny, nagging fear away, the one that had been eating at her all day. It tried to rear its ugly head, pointing out that here she was, alone. Just like the old days. She took a swallow of beer, knowing it wasn't at all like the old days. Because she knew Sam would be home. She smiled slightly as she tilted her head back, staring aimlessly at the darkening sky. Yes, she knew Sam would be home.

And a short time later, when she heard the front door slam shut, she let out a deep breath, relaxing—finally—because she wasn't alone any longer. And Sam found her quickly, the patio door sliding open as she stuck her head out.

"There you are." She slipped her hands around Tori's shoulders from behind for a tight hug. "God, I missed you today."

Tori turned, capturing a quick kiss from Sam before she released her. "I missed you too."

"Let me change," Sam said, squeezing Tori's arm as her hand slipped away. "I'd love a glass of wine," she called over her shoulder.

Tori nodded, her glance going one last time to the dark sky before going inside and closing the door.

She poured out the rest of her beer and filled two wineglasses, taking them into the bedroom, watching shamelessly as Sam stood there in nothing but her panties, searching for something warm to wear. Soon, she donned an oversized sweatshirt covering her small breasts, and Tori handed Sam her glass of wine.

"How long are you going to make me wait?" she finally asked.

Sam laughed. "For a recap of my first day? How boring would that be? I'd rather hear about your day." She linked arms with Tori and led her back into the living room. "Anything new with Father Michael?"

"Uh-huh. But you first."

Sam tucked her hair behind her ears, then sat cross-legged on the sofa, facing Tori. "I think Detective Travis—excuse me, *Lieutenant* Travis—is going to be wonderful. The job, however, is going to be boring as hell, I'm afraid. I spent most of the morning being introduced around." She leaned forward to touch Tori's leg. "And *yes*, I was Hunter's partner," she said with a smile. "I got that question a thousand times." She took a swallow of wine, then twirled the glass back and forth between her fingers. "The case I'm assigned to is money laundering. Apparently, how these cases work is, we get a tip from the FBI, CIU then does all the legwork and investigation, and the FBI gets to swoop in and make the arrests."

"What kind of money laundering?"

"Drugs. The phony company is some computer hardware place. They—or we—already know there's no inventory there, yet a lot of money changes hands each month. I really got in on the end of it though. The FBI is about to take it over."

"So no exciting homicides, huh?"

"No. And what's worse, they're sending me away for training." She reached over again and squeezed Tori's leg. "For three weeks, sweetheart."

"Three weeks? Where?"

"Los Angeles."

"*What?*"

"It's a program put on by the FBI. Travis says it's topnotch."

Tori felt the panic set in. "Three weeks?" she repeated.

"I know, Tori." She leaned closer, lightly kissing her on the lips. "I don't want to talk about it now, okay? It's going to come soon enough." She kissed her again. "Now, tell me about your day."

Tori leaned back, letting her breath out slowly. *Three weeks?* God, she'd die.

"Come on. Tell me how it went," Sam coaxed, her hand still lightly rubbing Tori's leg. "How was the new detective?"

Tori nodded and closed her eyes for a moment, then looked at Sam. "Three weeks?" It would be an eternity.

"Yes. Now, how was the new detective?"

"I'll die in three weeks."

"You will not." She sipped her wine. "You going to tell me or what?"

Tori sighed. "Casey O'Connor. Ever heard of her?"

Sam frowned. "Yeah. She got assigned to Assault after I left. I never met her though. What's she like?"

"She talks too much."

"I bet that was fun for you," Sam said with a laugh.

"Yeah. Loads of fun. But she got Alice Hagen to open up."

"You're kidding. So who was his lover?"

"We're going back in the morning. Her husband has a doctor's appointment. She said she'd talk then." Tori tapped Sam's leg. "But too little, too late. They're going to close the case this week. O'Connor says her captain actually told her that her involvement was just for show."

"Orders from the chief?"

"Yeah."

Sam shook her head. "This is going to come back and bite someone in the ass. Maybe not now, but someday, some reporter is going to be snooping around and someone's going to let slip what happened. I mean, what if he does get elected? Stevens, I mean. He'll have the interest of national media then. They'll dig. And out of the blue, some reporter will ask him about his brother. Then what?"

"Not our deal."

"So this O'Connor, she's just here for the week then?"

"I suppose. But she is having dinner with Marissa Goddard tonight."

"Oh, really? When did they meet?"

113

Tori smiled. "Tonight at dinner. Apparently Goddard is going to give her the spiel on why the case should be closed, and O'Connor is supposed to agree and sign off on it."

"So is she okay with it? O'Connor, I mean."

"No. That's why she's trying to get the housekeeper to talk. If we can find something else, then maybe the push to wrap things up will lessen. I mean, we all know Hidalgo did it."

"Which is only a small piece of the puzzle."

Tori nodded. "I just have this gut feeling that Hidalgo was really innocent in all this."

"What do you mean?"

"He's not a killer. I think he really was ordered to kill Father Michael." She finished her wine. "Blackmail maybe. Maybe something else. But I think someone told him to kill the priest, and then he got a bullet for his trouble."

"But that doesn't make sense, Tori. Like Ramirez said, if someone was willing to kill Hidalgo, why not just shoot Father Michael himself and not get a third party involved?"

"I don't know. There's too many ifs and maybes. We may never know what really happened."

CHAPTER SEVENTEEN

Casey stood on the corner outside the precinct, glancing at her watch for the third time. Marissa Goddard was five minutes late. Maybe she changed her mind. But Casey shook her head. She couldn't get that lucky. And if the woman turned out to be a carbon copy of Teresa Fillmore, it was going to be a short night anyway. She'd feign a headache if she needed to.

"O'Connor?"

Casey turned, her smile widening as an attractive woman approached. "Yes. I'm Casey O'Connor."

The woman held out her hand. "Marissa Goddard."

Casey stared, taking in the long, straight blond hair, tight-fitting black slacks and the red and black sweater. She looked back into expressive blue eyes, then arched one eyebrow. "*You're* Marissa Goddard?"

"Yes."

Casey laughed. "I'll kill her," she muttered as she took the offered hand, surprised at the firmness of the woman's handshake. *Teresa Fillmore my ass.*

"Excuse me?"

"It's just . . . nothing," she said. "Really nice to meet you, Ms. Goddard."

The woman nodded, then tucked her hair behind her ears impatiently. She motioned toward a silver Lincoln parked along the curb. "Shall we?"

Casey followed, her eyebrows shooting skyward as Marissa Goddard held the passenger door open for her.

"I'm in the mood for something spicy," Marissa said. "Perhaps you could recommend a good Tex-Mex place."

"Spicy? If it's spicy you want, I'm your woman."

"I'm sure you are. However, I was only talking about dinner."

"Well, so was I, Ms. Goddard. Whatever in the world did you think I meant?"

Their eyes held for a moment, then Marissa nodded, a slight smile on her face. "Call me Marissa."

Casey settled into the plush car, watching as Marissa went to the driver's side, her glance sliding briefly to Casey as she opened her door.

"I trust you're familiar with the case?"

Casey nodded. "Which makes me all the more confused as to why I'm here."

"What do you mean?"

"I'm Special Victims. And from everything I've read and heard, there was no sexual crime."

"Let me guess. You've been talking to Hunter."

"Yeah, five minutes with her and she had me brainwashed," she teased.

"No doubt."

"Take a left up here." Casey pointed. "And she didn't have to brainwash me. I read the reports. Facts are facts. But he was found naked. I guess that could be perceived as a sexual crime." She shrugged. "Or made to look that way."

"What are you insinuating, Detective O'Connor?"

"What makes you think I'm insinuating anything?"

"You're right. I'm sorry. I shouldn't judge you based on Hunter."

"At the light, turn left again." They were coming upon Casey's favorite restaurant. "And what's with you and Hunter?"

"We didn't exactly hit it off."

Casey laughed. "I guess I should have suspected that when I saw you."

"What do you mean?"

"I asked her what you looked like," Casey admitted. "She didn't exactly describe you correctly," she said, looking Marissa over top to bottom.

Marissa raised an eyebrow but said nothing.

Casey smiled. "You're attractive. Young."

"And this has what to do with Hunter?"

"She described you as fiftyish and a troll."

"A troll? That figures." She stopped at the light. "And fifty-ish? Surely I don't look fiftyish."

"I think Hunter was just giving me a hard time." She pointed down the street. "The Border."

"Border of the Sun? Doesn't sound very authentic. Is it a chain?"

"I thought you wanted spicy Tex-Mex, not authentic. And no, it's not a chain. Jose and Francesca Rios own it." Casey had known them for years.

Marissa pulled into the crowded parking lot, circling through twice before finding a spot. "Well, they're crowded, that's for sure. Perhaps we should try someplace else. We have things to discuss. I don't relish the idea of sitting in a noisy lobby with a crowd of people."

"We'll get a table, don't worry." Casey got out and slipped on the black leather jacket she'd had folded in her lap on the drive.

Marissa did the same, pulling a nearly identical one from the backseat.

"Nice jacket," Casey quipped as she fell into step beside her.

Marissa ignored her comment as she shoved her hands into her pockets. "The chief tells me the case will be wrapped up this week."

"Is that right?"

"Even though Hunter and Kennedy agreed that Juan Hidalgo was the killer, they refused to close the case without knowing the motive," Marissa said. "Quite frankly, I think that's silly."

"Silly? If a hit man takes out a federal judge, do you just file charges against the hit man? Or do you go after who hired him?"

"Juan Hidalgo was hardly a hit man. And what possible evidence could you have to indicate someone hired him?"

Casey held the door open, motioning Marissa inside. The smell of fresh tortillas and spicy food hit her the moment they walked in. People waiting to be seated crowded around the bar, some shouting out their drink requests over the noise.

"Hang on a sec," Casey said. She moved through the crowd, looking for a familiar face. She found her helping out at the cash register. She waited to the side until she was noticed. "Hello, Fran."

The older woman's eyes lit up. "Casey, welcome." Francesca slid around the counter, both hands reaching out to grasp Casey's arms. "So good to see you again." She looked past her. "You have a date, yes?"

Casey chuckled. "Not exactly. A working date," she said. "Any chance I can get a table?"

"Of course, Casey. For you, I find a nice spot."

"Thanks, Fran. Let me go find Marissa."

"Ah, Marissa," she said, her Spanish accent rolling the *r* nicely. "Sounds lovely."

"She's lovely to look at, yes," Casey said. "But it's business."

"So you say, Casey. Go get this business date. I shall see."

Casey bent to kiss her cheek. "Thanks. Be right back."

Marissa met her with an amused smile. "The owner?"

"Yeah. Wonderful woman. She's going to get us a table." Casey politely took Marissa's elbow only to have the other woman stop and turn and look quickly at the hand touching her arm.

"I appreciate the chivalry, Detective, but it's certainly not necessary. I'm not in the need of an escort this evening."

"Damn. Me and my manners, what was I thinking," Casey said lightly. "I'll let you fight your own way through the crowd then."

And she did, turning toward the dining room and looking for Francesca. Maybe Hunter was right. Marissa was attractive, yeah. But arrogant and obnoxious weren't a stretch. She found Fran waiting for her in a quiet corner, away from the noise.

"How's this?" Francesca gestured.

"Perfect."

"And your lady friend?"

Casey turned, waiting as Marissa wound her way through the tables. "Fran, meet Marissa Goddard. Marissa, this is Francesca Rios, creator of the best chicken enchiladas you will ever eat."

Francesca bowed her head politely as she pulled out a chair for Marissa. "Welcome, Marissa. Always nice to meet a new lady friend of Casey's." She winked subtly at Casey before squeezing her shoulder. "I will send someone over to take your order. Margaritas are on me tonight, Casey."

Casey grinned as Fran walked away, then curbed it when Marissa glared at her. "She thinks I'm your date?"

Casey shrugged. "Trust me, you could do a lot worse." She folded her hands together on the table and leaned closer. "I'm considered a good catch." She raised her eyebrows teasingly before settling back again.

Marissa finally relaxed. "I suppose I should be thankful it's not Hunter I'm having dinner with."

"I kinda like her," Casey said. "I was told she was obnoxious and arrogant for a woman." Then she laughed. "Which is pretty much how Hunter described you."

"She's abrasive."

"Yeah, she may have used that word too."

Marissa opened her menu and scanned it. "Kennedy is a doll. I can't believe she's with someone like Hunter."

"Oh, I don't know. Tori's got that tall, dark and handsome thing down pretty good. And I've not met Kennedy." She glanced up as a waiter approached and promptly placed a basket of hot tortilla chips and both red and green salsa in front of them. "If you like your margaritas with a kick, you've got to try the Rios Rita. It's the best in town."

"You're a police officer and I'm driving. What are you advocating?"

"One margarita with your meal should be fine, Ms. Goddard. And if you're concerned, I'll be happy to take the wheel." She said to the waiter, "Two Rios Ritas. I'll have mine on the rocks." She looked at Marissa with eyebrows raised.

"The same."

"Excellent choice," he said as he bowed courteously. "May I get you an appetizer this evening?"

Marissa shook her head. "None for me, thanks."

"Very well. Your drinks will be right out."

Casey reached for a chip and scooped up the green sauce, pausing to drip the excess off before popping it into her mouth. "Fabulous," she murmured as she chewed. "The red is hotter than the green." She grinned. "And being a Yankee and all, you might want to take it easy on the salsa."

Marissa took a chip from the basket and broke it in half, then dipped one into the red salsa. "Your Yankee comment doesn't offend me, Detective," she said, taking a bite. "I'm from

Southern California."

Casey laughed. "Damn. But I should have known that. Long blond hair, nice tan," she said. "But they told me you were from Boston."

Marissa nodded as she dipped the other half of her chip into the green salsa. "I've been in Boston the last eight years. I keep meaning to move back to the West Coast but there never seems to be enough time. And a tanning bed works wonders." She reached for her water. "I think the green is hotter."

"Wimp." Casey took another chip. "So, do you have somebody back home? In Boston?" she asked, then leaned back as the waiter brought their drinks. "Thanks."

Marissa stared across the table, meeting her eyes. "This isn't really a date, you know. We're supposed to be discussing the case."

"Yeah, but then we'll just end up arguing and ruin our meal. How about we discuss the case after dinner? Because if I had to guess, this is the first time you've had a chance to get out and relax in over a week."

Marissa nodded. "My dinner dates have been with the mayor and his wife twice, the mayor and chief once, Monsignor Bernard from the diocese once and the rest alone."

"And isn't this more fun?"

Marissa smiled. "Yes. Thank you, it is."

Casey took a sip from her drink, her eyes closing, enjoying the perfect mix of sweet and sour. "God, that's good." She looked at Marissa as she tasted hers. "Yes?"

Marissa's eyes widened as she swallowed. "Wow." She cleared her throat. "I may have to take you up on the driving offer. That's stout."

Casey reached for the chips again. "So? You got someone? Back home?" she asked again.

Marissa shook her head. "Not anymore. I did." She paused. "I had a perfect life and a perfect job making tons of money.

Bethany was everything I'd always wanted." She sipped again from her drink. "And she loved me. But she wanted everything, you know. She wanted a normal life, she wanted kids." Marissa laughed. "And she wanted me to have them. I can play the traditional girl," she said, pointing at herself, "but I never had the desire to have kids. I'm not exactly mother material." She tilted her head. "It didn't matter. She left me." She opened her purse and pulled out a cigarette, then looked for an ashtray.

"No smoking."

"I hate these new laws." She tossed her cigarette down just as the waiter approached again.

"Are we ready to order, ladies?"

"Chicken enchiladas with extra sour cream," Casey said quickly, knowing exactly what she wanted. "With black beans."

"Hungry?" Marissa asked as she looked back at her menu.

"Starved."

"Mmm. I'll have the combo enchiladas. Chicken, beef and veggie," she said. "And black beans also."

"Combo is good too," Casey said, scooping up another chip. "So tell me what happened."

"With?"

"Bethany. You said she left you."

"What? You actually want details?"

"Sure. Why not?"

Marissa leaned forward. "Why are we having dinner and conversation like we're old friends?"

Casey shrugged. "I'm friendly."

"I'm not."

Casey laughed. "Okay. I was a psychology major."

"That means what?"

"I'm nosy. And I ask a lot of questions." She grabbed another chip. "So? She left you. Why?"

Marissa sighed. "I was never there."

"You travel around putting out church fires a lot, do you?"

"Not just church fires, no. We specialize in media relations. And we're good. You remember Trinity Oil?"

"Trinity? You call that good? Half the higher-ups got prison time." The sentences hadn't been light, Casey recalled.

"Well, can you imagine how it would have been if we'd not been there? We also did Senator Bailey when he got that intern pregnant. We managed the mine disaster in Kentucky after the explosion. And yeah, we do church fires. When the Boston diocese had all that trouble, we were there." She drank the last of her margarita. "And one time when I was gone for about six months, Bethany's phone calls got less and less. The last month or so, we existed through voice mail. And when I got home, the place was empty."

"Empty? What? She took everything?"

"No. Empty of life. She didn't take anything except our dog."

"And you didn't try to find her?"

"Of course. But there was no fairytale ending. She'd quit her job and moved to Hartford."

Casey frowned. "Where?"

"It's in Connecticut. I swear—you Texans. There's a whole world out there, you know."

Casey smiled. "So they say."

"Anyway, she's seeing someone now. Someone normal, someone with a real job."

"A real job?"

"Someone who's around. I called her once, just to let her know there weren't any hard feelings, just to let her know I was happy for her."

Casey nodded. "Closure?"

Marissa sighed. "Not really. She told me not to call again."

"So let me guess. You've given up on relationships, you limit your involvement both personally and professionally, and you satisfy your intimacy needs by having unfulfilling sex with people you don't really like." She raised her eyebrows. "Am I right?"

"You're very perceptive, Detective O'Connor." She leaned closer. "But I wouldn't really call it unfulfilling sex. It's actually quite refreshing not to have to worry about all that emotional crap that goes along with having a relationship." She sat back and twirled her empty glass. "And what about you, Detective? Do you have someone waiting at home?"

"Me?" Casey laughed. "No, no. I'm career-oriented. For right now, at least. I tried mixing the two, but I was told I was incapable of having a mature relationship," she said, surprised that there was still a hint of bitterness in her voice. So she laughed it away. "A long time ago."

"So you get by with unfulfilling sex with people you don't really like?"

"Therein lies the difference. I'm not afraid of involvement like you are. It's just that now is not the right time for me. I want to focus on my career. So I get by with the occasional fling." She smiled. "*Occasional* being the key word."

She looked up as the waiter approached with their dinner, waiting patiently as her chicken enchiladas were placed in front of her.

"Another drink?" he asked.

Casey shook her head. "Better not. Thank you."

"And for you?"

Marissa also shook her head. "Water is fine."

"Well, enjoy your meal, ladies. Let me know if you need anything else."

"Looks great," Marissa said when he left. "Smells great."

"Tastes great," Casey murmured around a mouthful. "I could eat here every day."

Marissa nodded as she took her first bite. "Excellent."

Casey took a swallow of water, then pointed at Marissa. "Okay, so let me get this straight. You're here—your job—is to make sure Father Michael's affair is not made public—"

"Alleged affair," Marissa interrupted.

"Right. Alleged affair. Sorry." She put her fork down. "So you're here to make sure the *alleged* affair stays under wraps. You want the case closed, Hidalgo tabbed for the murder, Father Michael voted into sainthood and all's well with the world when you head back to Boston."

Marissa laughed. "That's pretty much it. Can you make it happen?"

"Well, you may get your wish. The brass wants this case closed by the end of the week."

"Then why do I get the feeling you're going to spend the next four days trying to prove me wrong?"

Casey smiled. "Because it's my job. But I have no doubt *this* case will end the way you want."

"This case?"

"Yeah. Everyone seems to forget that Hidalgo's murderer is still out there. And I can assure you, Tori Hunter won't let that one go cold."

Marissa rested her elbows on the table and folded her hands together. "I would assume if she's told to let it go, she would. I mean, she does follow orders, right?"

Casey shook her head. "No way. If Homicide is ordered to drop it, it'll just scream cover-up. Hunter will go nuts."

Marissa scooped up a forkful of rice. "How well do you know her?"

"Hunter? Oh, I just met her this morning. But she's intense. I think she's all about honor, about the truth." She paused. "About doing the right thing. No way she drops this case."

"So is this your psychology degree paying off again?"

Casey attacked the last of her enchiladas. "Yeah. Comes in handy, doesn't it?"

"I'm curious about one thing."

"Shoot."

"You don't seem surprised by any of this. The so-called cover-up. You haven't asked me who could be involved."

Casey raised an eyebrow teasingly. "Oh? You think I don't already know?"

"Do you?"

"Sorry. Top secret. Can't tell."

Marissa nodded. "I wouldn't have thought Hunter would trust you so soon. Not enough to tell you what she knew."

"Well, time is short." Casey stabbed at the last of her beans. "And I *am* very trustworthy."

"I'll have to take your word for it. I doubt I'll be around long enough to find out."

"You're leaving already?"

"As soon as the case is closed. I expect to be back in Boston by the weekend."

"That's a shame. And here I was going to invite you out on the town." Casey shoved her plate away. "We may not come close to agreeing about this case, but I find you really attractive," she admitted.

Marissa laughed. "Oh, my God. You're hitting on me?"

"Call it what you like."

Marissa leaned forward. "I'm not going to sleep with you."

Casey smiled, their eyes meeting. "I haven't asked you yet."

CHAPTER EIGHTEEN

"So, are you going to tell me or what?" Tori's curiosity was killing her.

"Tell you what?" Casey pointed up ahead. "Pull in here. I'm starving."

Hunter pulled into the drive-thru lane, quietly shaking her head. *How could she possibly eat as much as she did?* "Think how much time we'd save if you ate breakfast at home."

"That'd mean there'd have to be food there." Casey handed her a ten. "Get me the sausage and egg sandwich, hash browns and a large coffee."

"Sure that's all? Don't want a biscuit on the side?"

Casey shook her head. "Better not. Had a big meal last night." She smiled. "You know, with Marissa."

"And again, are you going to tell me what happened?"

"Nothing happened, Hunter. We had a nice dinner, talked

about the case, flirted a little, and then she said she wasn't going to sleep with me."

Tori stared at her. "Are you crazy? You want to *sleep* with her?"

"Despite your description of her, I found her quite attractive. A bit arrogant, yes, but I even found that attractive."

"Been a while for you, has it?"

Casey laughed. "Damn, Hunter, you're making a joke. And here everyone said you were all business."

Tori shrugged. "Sam says I've mellowed."

"Speaking of Sam, Marissa thinks she's a doll. She's not quite sure what Sam sees in you, though."

Tori pulled up to the window and gave Casey's order, then tossed a glance at her. She was about to say she didn't give a shit what Marissa Goddard thought, but she stopped herself. Then she blurted out the one thing that was foremost on her mind. "Sam's leaving."

Casey frowned. "What? Oh, man, I'm sorry. What happened?"

Tori shook her head. "No, I mean she's leaving for a training session. For three weeks."

"Well, shit, Hunter, I thought you meant she was leaving you."

Tori stared straight ahead. "Feels like it," she said quietly.

"What's up? You guys having problems?"

"No, no. It's just, well, we've never been apart." Tori turned as Casey's breakfast was handed through the window. "Thanks."

Casey took the bag and ripped into it. "You didn't get you any coffee, Hunter?"

"Already had some." She pulled away, watching as Casey took a huge bite from her sandwich. "How do you stay so thin?"

"Blessed. My grandmother was a pole bean," she said as she sampled the hash browns. "So when is Sam leaving?"

Tori sighed. "Tomorrow."

"Damn. For three weeks, huh?"

"Yep."

"Where do you live, anyway?"

"Over near White Rock."

"Well, hell, Hunter, if I'm not busy with Marissa this weekend, we can hang out."

"Hang out?"

"Yeah. Have a few beers somewhere, catch a movie or something."

Tori glanced at her quickly, then back at the road. "You fish?"

"Used to fish all the time. My grandfather lived out on Lake Fork. Had a nice bass boat." She grabbed her coffee as Tori took the corner too fast. "Have I told you your driving sucks?"

"He still out there?" Tori asked, ignoring the dig.

"No. He died on Christmas Eve, two years ago." She shrugged. "My brother got the boat."

"And?"

"And we don't get along." She wadded up her trash and put it in the bag, then tossed it to the back of Tori's Explorer.

"Why don't you get along?"

"Come on, Hunter, we're not going to have a heart-to-heart, are we?"

Tori smiled. "Yeah, what was I thinking? I don't really do heart-to-hearts." She turned onto the Hagens' street. "But I've got a boat out on Eagle Mountain Lake. Not a bass boat—it's a cabin cruiser. But I wouldn't mind company if you wanted to do a little fishing."

Casey grinned. "Absolutely. And even if I did score a date with Marissa, I'd probably turn her down for a chance to fish."

Tori pulled along the curb and parked, noting the drawn drapes in the Hagens' house. "Early Saturday. We'll make a day of it." She got out, thinking Sam would be proud of her. She wasn't going to go into a shell and hide until Sam came back. She'd promised her that. And O'Connor? Well, they seemed to get along fine, and it'd been a while since Tori had added a new friend to her life.

"Looks kinda quiet," Casey said. "You think she bailed on us?"

"Maybe." Tori rang the doorbell, then knocked several times when she heard no sound.

"Damn. And I thought we had her too."

Tori pressed her face against the window, trying to see inside. She rapped loudly on the pane. "Mrs. Hagen?" she called. "Police. Open up."

"She must have gone to the doctor with her husband."

Tori shook her head. "I don't think so. She wanted to tell us. She wanted to clear her conscience." She moved off the porch and around to the side of the house.

"She slept on it, changed her mind," Casey said as she followed her. "Where the hell are you going?"

"To the back."

The wood of the privacy fence was weathered and worn but sturdy. Tori gripped the top, testing it.

"You're going over?"

"The gate's locked."

"Don't we need a warrant for this?"

Tori rolled her eyes, then pulled herself over the fence and dropped to the ground on the other side. She waited. "Are you coming or what?"

"I'm coming, I'm coming." Casey gripped the top of the fence, mimicking Tori as she scampered over the top and landed lightly on the ground beside her. "You're not too bad for an old lady, Hunter."

Tori scowled but said nothing as she crept silently to the back porch. The blinds were pulled up in the kitchen, the morning sunlight streaming inside. Tori followed the light, her eyes widening when she saw Mrs. Hagen.

"Goddamn," she murmured as she pulled her gun from the

holster.

Casey pulled her weapon too, following Tori's gaze into the kitchen. "Oh, no."

Tori turned the doorknob and found it locked. She looked at Casey and shook her head, then used her shoulder to break the lower windowpane in the door.

"I'll call for backup."

"No need for that," Tori said as she reached through the glass to unlock the door.

They walked into the kitchen, Tori staring at the floor where a pool of blood surrounded Alice Hagen's head, her perfectly coiffed hair now damp and matted. Her eyes were opened staring lifelessly at the ceiling of her pristine kitchen. Tori motioned silently to the den, then pointed at Casey, who nodded.

Tori then walked down the hallway toward the bedrooms, finding them quiet and empty. "Clear," she called.

"All clear," Casey answered from the other room.

Tori flipped open her phone, dialing Malone's number as she came back into the kitchen. "It's me," she said when he answered. "Alice Hagen's been shot."

"What the hell? Dead?"

"Afraid so. Looks similar to Hidalgo. Shot to the head. No sign of forced entry. In fact, the house was locked. We broke in through the kitchen window in the back."

"Broke in? Please say there was probable cause, Hunter," Malone said.

Tori flicked her gaze at Casey. "Now, come on, Lieutenant, you don't think I'd do something illegal, do you?"

"Well, Sam's not there to rein you in, so who the hell knows. Sikes! Get in here," he yelled and Tori pulled the phone away from her ear with a grimace. "Sit tight, Hunter. I'll notify the crime lab. Maybe we'll get lucky."

Tori looked back at the spotless kitchen. "Maybe."

"And Sikes got the report from Mac on the fingerprints. Only one unaccounted for."

"Why? Didn't they print everyone?"

"Everyone on the list, yeah. Apparently our mystery prints weren't on the list."

"How convenient," she murmured.

"I'm going to send Sikes over there. I want you and what's-her-name from Special Victims—"

"O'Connor," Tori supplied.

"Right. O'Connor. I want you two at the church. Get some reaction on the housekeeper, see if they left someone off the list, whatever. I'll let the captain know. Maybe they'll lighten up on us closing the case."

"All right."

"But don't hold your breath, Hunter. Chief wants this wrapped up nice and tidy by Friday. I doubt the murder of a housekeeper will change his mind."

Tori slammed her phone closed, just barely resisting the urge to fling it across the room. "Goddamn politics." She looked at Casey. "He doesn't think this will have a bearing on the case. Chief wants it over and done with by Friday."

"How the hell can we close it?" Casey yelled. "A goddamn potential witness is shot dead." She pointed at Alice Hagen. "Shot dead right here."

"Don't yell at me. I'm not the one who wants it closed," Tori snapped.

Casey shook her head. "We killed her, Hunter. We goddamn killed her," she said, her voice lower now.

"What the fuck are you talking about?"

"She knew. And we kept pushing her and pushing her. So when she was about to give up a name, they kill her instead."

"How the hell would someone know she was about to tell us a name?"

"Maybe they were watching her, watching us. Maybe they knew you and Kennedy had been here before. Hell, maybe she

132

told them because she freaked."

"Come on, O'Connor. Who the hell is she going to tell?"

"She's goddamn shot in the head! She told someone something." Casey paced the room, her glance going again and again to Alice Hagen. As if seeing for the first time, Casey peered at the worn rosary beads still wrapped between her fingers. "Christ, Hunter, how do you do this all the time?"

"What?"

"Homicide." Casey looked up. "Like I said, most of my victims are still alive when I get to them."

Tori shook her head. "If your unit had been up and running last year, your victims would have been dead. Raped, mutilated, murdered," Tori said quietly, remembering.

"Yeah, I know. It's what prompted them to bring us up earlier than we were ready, I think. Hell, Hunter, I worked Assault for a while, I saw my share of abuse, you know. But I'm glad that case still fell to Homicide."

Tori sighed. "Malone wants us at the church. He's sending Sikes over to cover this one."

"It should be us," Casey protested. "This is our case."

"We'll find the answers at the church, not here. Maybe it'll give you a chance to work on your moves with Marissa Goddard. Work on that date you're trying to get with her."

Casey shook her head, glancing again to Alice Hagen. "I can't believe the bastard killed her."

"Well, believe it."

CHAPTER NINETEEN

"You have her cell number?" Tori asked incredulously. Casey was dialing as they walked along the sidewalk to the church. "I don't have her number. Why do you have her number?"

Casey grinned. "You didn't flirt with her, obviously."

"As if," Tori murmured.

"Hey, Marissa. It's Casey." She winked at Tori. "Got a minute for me?" She paused. "Well, me and Hunter. She misses you," she said with a laugh.

Tori rolled her eyes and nudged Casey with her elbow. "Get on with it."

"Thanks. We'll be right up."

She closed her phone. "She'll make time for us. Even with you along," she said with her own nudge. "But let me do the talking." Then she paused. "If it's all right with you, of course."

Tori nodded. "It's all yours, hotshot. I'll just tag along."

"And you'll be able to hold your temper?"

"What temper? I don't have a temper?"

"Oh, God, Hunter, it was the main thing they warned me about."

"They? They who?"

"Everybody, Hunter. Everybody." Casey stopped, turning to straighten Tori's jacket collar. "Now you're presentable."

"Thanks. And remember, don't accuse," Tori reminded her as they entered the main lobby of the diocese office. "We won't get anywhere if you accuse."

"I won't accuse." She went to the reception desk. "Marissa Goddard is expecting us. Detectives O'Connor and Hunter," she said. "Special Victims." She glanced at Hunter. "And Homicide."

"Of course. You may go into the sitting area. I'll call her."

Casey nodded, then looked around. "Sitting area?" she whispered to Tori.

"This way," Tori said, motioning with her head. "Very impressive. Lots of paintings."

Casey eyed the plush burgundy carpet, and then she stopped, looking around at the religious paintings on the wall. "Damn, Hunter," she whispered. "Kinda spooky in here. It's too quiet."

Tori nodded. "That was pretty much my impression, yeah."

"You think they're real?" she asked, motioning to the paintings.

"Of course they're real, O'Connor."

Casey moved closer. "What do you think they're worth?"

"Sorry. Don't have a clue." Tori leaned against the wall. "Maybe you can ask Marissa. You know, in one of those quiet moments you're hoping to have."

Casey laughed. "Careful, Hunter. If you keep up the teasing, you're going to ruin your reputation. I was told you didn't have a lighter side."

Tori shrugged. "It comes and goes."

Casey walked around the room, absently inspecting each painting as they waited for Marissa. Tori glanced at her watch. It had been ten minutes.

"Surely she can't be that busy," Casey said. "You think she's doing this on purpose?"

Tori smiled. "You think, O'Connor?"

"Yeah, well, she's not making any points with me."

"Maybe—" But Tori's reply died when she heard Marissa Goddard's footsteps on the marble floor down the hallway. "That'll be her."

They both turned, watching as Marissa came into the room, her glance going from one to the other.

"Detectives," she greeted with a slight nod. "To what do I owe this pleasure?"

Casey moved forward. "Now, see, I knew you would find it pleasurable to see me again." She gestured to Tori. "Wasn't sure about Hunter here, though."

"I see you haven't left your sense of humor at the restaurant, O'Connor." She turned to Tori. "How is Samantha? I hear she has a new position."

Tori raised an eyebrow. "Is there anything you don't know?"

"Not if I can help it, no. Now, what can I help you with today?"

Casey said, "A couple of things. One, they got the prints matched. All but one." She stared at her. "Any idea who that one could be?"

Marissa shook her head. "The list of names came from Monsignor Bernard and Sister Margaret. I think the house-keeper, Alice Hagen, contributed a couple as well. She knew a lot about the comings and goings."

"Yeah. She probably knew a lot. She probably knew who Father Michael was sleeping with and everything."

"Allegedly," Marissa corrected.

"Well, she's allegedly dead."

"*What?* Alice Hagen?"

Casey nodded. "Shot in the head. We found her this morning."

"Oh, my God," Marissa murmured. She looked around, then motioned for them to follow her. "Let's go into my office. We can talk in private."

"You have an office?" Tori asked, surprised.

"Temporary, yes. I hope to be gone by the weekend."

"Not likely," Tori said. "We have no intention of closing the case."

Marissa stopped and turned around. "I wasn't aware it was your call, Detective."

"I doubt even the chief would order the case closed with all these loose ends."

Marissa smiled. "Don't worry, Hunter. It's *really* not your call." She opened a door down the hallway and motioned them inside. "Have a seat."

"So I guess no one here's been notified about Alice Hagen yet?" Casey asked.

"No. At least I wasn't aware of the situation. I'll need to brief Monsignor Bernard. What happened exactly?"

Tori and Casey exchanged glances, then Tori nodded, giving Casey the okay to talk.

"We had an appointment with her this morning," Casey said. "She was going to give up the name."

"The name?"

"The name of Father Michael's lover."

"Give me a break, O'Connor," Marissa scoffed.

"I'm serious. We went to see her yesterday. She was about to tell us but her husband came in. She told us to come back this morning when her husband would be at his doctor's appointment."

"And we showed up and found her dead," Tori finished. "Shot in the head, just like Juan Hidalgo."

"So naturally you assume the two murders are related."

"Naturally."

Marissa leaned forward, looking at Casey. "You really think she was going to give up a name?"

"Yes. Absolutely."

Marissa leaned back again, her gaze going from Casey to Tori. She shook her head. "But it doesn't really matter, does it? No matter what you dig up, Father Michael's case is closed."

"It doesn't matter that a woman is dead?" Tori asked loudly. "Of course it does."

"The case is still closed, Detective."

"If you think the media is so easily swayed here, you're crazy," Tori said. "We can close the case on Father Michael, but his accused killer is dead, and now his housekeeper is dead. You think just closing Father Michael's case will make those others go away?"

"But you see, that's not my problem. My only concern is Father Michael's reputation. And as long as it is not soiled, then my job is done. If they want to scrutinize the police department for the other two murders, that's not my concern."

"As I told you once before, don't think I won't go to the media."

"And as I told you, Hunter, don't even try to threaten me. This is way over your head."

Casey stood up. "Will you two knock it off?" She paced the room. "Think about it. A very nice grandmother just got killed because she knew something, because she was about to talk to us." She looked at Marissa. "Where does it end? Who else knows something? Who else is in danger?"

"You're being overly dramatic, Detective."

"Am I? Then whose goddamn name was left off the list?"

"I told you I don't know." Marissa shifted in her chair. "I was told they came up with twenty or so names of who they thought could have been in the rectory in the last month. And why do you assume a name was left off? If the thirteenth print is indeed the killer's, why would you believe the church would know it anyway?"

Tori's laugh was humorless. "Come on, Goddard. It's not the killer's. Hidalgo is the killer, remember. The thirteenth print belongs to his lover."

"Again, Hunter, it's just one big circle. You already know who Father Michael's killer was. Why is it so important that you know who his lover was?"

Tori smiled. "Don't you mean *alleged* lover?"

"Of course."

"And it's important because the lover could be the one responsible for the murders."

"Or the lover could be next on the list," Casey added.

Marissa shook her head. "You two are crazy." She held up her hands. "What list? You think there's a hit list or something? Jesus Christ, a priest was murdered," she shouted. "That's it. End of story. There's no hit list. There's no revenge. Juan Hidalgo killed Father Michael. Period."

Casey stared at her. "But why?" she asked quietly. "Why would he kill him?"

"Who knows? Maybe he just didn't like him."

"So who killed Juan?" Casey pressed her.

"Not my problem, O'Connor. Yours."

Casey smiled. "Well, technically, it's Hunter's problem," she said, tossing a glance at Tori. "I'm just kinda tagging along." She leaned over Marissa's desk, resting her palms on the glass. "Don't you care even a little bit? Don't you care that Alice Hagen got killed this morning? Don't you want to know *why?*"

Marissa looked at them and Tori saw a moment of weakness there, a moment of indecision, then nothing but indifference as the mask slipped back into place.

"It's not my job to *care*, Detective. And no, I don't want to know why."

"Damn." Casey straightened to her full height. "Are you even human?" She didn't wait for an answer. She walked toward the door, then paused. "Come on, Hunter. We're wasting our time here."

"When will I get the reports on Mrs. Hagen?" Marissa called as they headed out.

Tori turned back around. "Not our problem."

CHAPTER TWENTY

Tori walked into their apartment, surprised that Sam beat her home. The smell of Chinese food greeted her and she went into the kitchen, inspecting the containers on the counter.

"Is that you?" Sam called from the bedroom.

Tori smiled. "Who else have you given a key to?" she asked as she opened one of the containers.

"Stay out of the shrimp," Sam warned her.

Tori popped one into her mouth before closing the box again. "Okay." *Delicious.* She opened the fridge and pulled out the bottle of wine they'd started last evening. She uncorked it easily and filled two glasses, then went in search of Sam. Stopping in the doorway of their bedroom, she watched as Sam tossed clothes into the nearly full piece of luggage that lay on the bed.

"Thanks," Sam said, reaching for the wine. "I need this. I need lots of this."

"Taking a lot of clothes," Tori observed.

"I'm sure we'll have a chance to do laundry at some point, I just want to have enough for the first week." Sam clinked her glass with Tori's. "You're going to be okay, aren't you?"

"Sure. In fact, I already have a date for Saturday." Tori nodded, not sure at all.

Sam smiled. "Good. On the boat?"

"Yeah. I asked O'Connor. Turns out she likes to fish."

"Wonderful. It would do you good to make a new friend." Sam took a sip of her wine.

"Yeah. She's all right."

"So how did it go today?"

Tori looked away. "It sucked. Alice Hagen, we found her dead this morning."

"Oh, my God. What happened?"

"Shot."

"Oh, no." Sam's eyes widened. "Surely they won't close the case now?"

"We haven't heard otherwise. Malone said they were still going to make an official announcement by Friday. Case closed."

"I just can't believe it. I guess short of the bishop getting killed, these murders aren't going to be linked." Sam sighed. "I'm sorry, Tori. I feel so terrible about Mrs. Hagen."

"I know. It was quite a shock." Tori glanced at the pile of clothes Sam had packed. A lot of clothes. "You're coming back, right?" She intended the question as a joke, of course. But the words hung in the room as they stared at each other.

Sam's eyes softened. "You know, I was thinking," she said as she took Tori's wineglass from her. "While I'm gone, maybe you could clean out your apartment. Bring whatever you want to keep over here."

"You were thinking that, huh?"

Sam slipped her hands under Tori's sweater, caressing her sides. "You don't need it anymore," she said softly. "This is home now. With me. So, yes, I'm coming back."

Tori closed her eyes. "I'm scared," she whispered.

"I know. But you don't need to be. You don't ever need to be scared again." Sam moved her lips across Tori's face and Tori trembled as Sam's hands slid higher, resting just below Tori's breasts. "This is home," she said again. "And I'll be back before you know it."

Tori opened her eyes, finding Sam's. "I don't want you to go."

"And I would do anything to stay." She cupped Tori's breasts, which made Tori gasp. "I love you. And you love me. And that's all that matters."

"Yes," Tori whispered.

She pulled Sam to her, flush against her body as their mouths met. No matter how many months passed, no matter how many times they touched, how many times they made love, the intensity was still there, the want—the *need*—was still there. And her body trembled as it always did when Sam's soft hands moved across her skin.

"Make love to me," Sam murmured against her lips. "Would you please?"

Unceremoniously, Tori tossed the luggage to the floor, pulling Sam with her to the bed. She slid Sam's shirt up, exposing her small breasts. She closed her eyes for a moment, then opened them. "I love you," she whispered as her mouth found Sam's swollen nipple.

CHAPTER TWENTY-ONE

Casey slammed the phone down. "Damn, but that woman is hot. There's just something about her. She's got that angry, sarcastic tone this morning, you know."

"Does she have any other tone?" Tori asked, surprised at how comfortable she felt having Casey occupy Sam's old desk.

"Don't you think she's hot?"

Tori shuddered. "I do not think Marissa Goddard is hot, no."

"She could make a grown man cry." Casey grinned. "Wonder what she'd do to a woman?"

"Do you really want to find out?"

Casey wiggled her eyebrows. "Yeah. I really want to find out."

Tori leaned forward. "She's scary."

"Yeah, but—"

"Hey, you two, get in here," Malone called from his doorway. "Sikes, you too."

"What do you think is going on?" Casey whispered.

"It's Friday. Deadline day."

"But I'm still working on Marissa."

"Well, you should've worked faster."

"Come on, ladies," Sikes said. "Let's get this over with."

"Did Mac get anything at the Hagens' house?" Casey asked.

"Clean. No usable prints."

"We can't catch a break on anything, can we?" Tori said.

"Sit down, people," Malone said. "This won't take long."

Tori took a seat. "They're actually closing it?"

"Yeah, Hunter, they're closing it. And Marissa Goddard gets the privilege of making the announcement. I hear the chief is going to make a statement as well," he said matter-of-factly as he tidied some papers on his desk. "It has been proven that Juan Hidalgo murdered Father Michael. Cause of death was strangulation."

"What about Hidalgo's murder?" Sikes asked. "I still have no leads there."

Malone sighed. "Hidalgo's murder is a separate case and has no bearing on this one. There is no physical evidence to link the two."

"And Alice Hagen?" Tori asked.

"Alice Hagen has no link to Father Michael."

"Ballistic evidence shows it was the same gun, Lieutenant. How the hell can they ignore that?"

"As I said, Hunter, there is no physical evidence to link Alice Hagen to Father Michael. Juan Hidalgo is not a part of the equation."

"The hell he's not," Tori said furiously. "How can you go along with a goddamn cover-up?"

Malone pounded his fist on his desk. "Do not use that word, Hunter. I am following orders, just like you are going to follow orders. Now the case is closed. Period."

"But what about—"

"Hunter, please, it's out of my hands. Don't you think I'd do something if I could?"

"It makes no goddamn sense."

"I know it makes no goddamn sense, Hunter," he said, his voice equally as loud as hers. "But we work the cases that are given to us." He pointed at O'Connor. "Special Victims gets to close the case on Father Michael. We still have two open homicides here, Hunter." He nodded. "We work what's given to us." He stared at them for a moment, waiting. "If there are no questions, I'd like to officially thank Detective O'Connor for her assistance in this case. I believe the chief will also address Special Victims' involvement with it." He tidied the papers on his desk one last time, then set them aside. "Hunter, if I could have a word with you," he said as he dismissed Sikes and O'Connor.

"Well, I'm going to split, guys. Can't say it's been fun." Casey shook hands with Sikes. "I'll expect an invite to the next poker party." She glanced at Tori. "We still on for tomorrow, Hunter?"

"Early. Come by the house."

Casey nodded. "Lieutenant, I'd say it's been a pleasure, but frankly, this case sucked."

"Same here, O'Connor." He waited until they were gone before eyeing Tori, speaking before she could. "It is what it is, Hunter."

She nodded. "I know."

He motioned toward the squad room. "She okay?"

"O'Connor? Yeah, she's good." Tori smiled. "She talks too much."

"Her captain thinks highly of her. Off the record, Hunter, we're all in agreement on this case, you know. But our hands are tied."

"I understand."

"No, you don't. Hell, you don't understand it anymore than I do. But nobody's got answers for us." He scowled. "This is bigger than just a murder. I know it and you know it. But it ends here."

"And if our investigation of the deaths of Hidalgo and Hagen shed light on it?"

"Then we'll just have to see how far they'll go, won't we."

Tori narrowed her eyes. "What do you know, Stan?"

"I'm not stupid and neither are you. If the mayor's office is involved, if the chief is involved, then it's politics, plain and simple. I don't know why, and I don't know who's trying to hide what, but it's politics."

Tori nodded. Malone was just guessing. She knew it to be fact, but she wasn't willing to break Sam's confidence by sharing what she knew.

"By the way, I hear Kennedy got shipped out."

"That's one way of putting it. Three weeks. Gonna be kinda quiet around the house."

"You gonna be okay?"

"Yeah. I mean, we talk on the phone. It's not like we won't communicate for three weeks."

"And O'Connor?"

"What about her?"

"New friend?"

"Oh, you mean tomorrow? Yeah, she likes to fish. We're going out to the boat."

Malone nodded. "Good, Hunter, good." He laughed. "Because Sam told me to keep an eye on you."

CHAPTER TWENTY-TWO

Casey pulled the collar of her leather jacket tighter against her neck, trying to ward off the cold that had settled on the city. Apparently the few days of early spring were only a tease. She glanced skyward, wondering if they'd have to cancel their fishing trip.

"Damn," she whispered as a gust of wind hit her face.

She jogged up the steps to the diocese, the door closing gently behind her as she shivered in the sudden warmth. She put on her most charming smile for the young woman behind the desk.

"Where did this come from?" she asked, motioning out the window.

"Well, it is still winter," she said. "We might get freezing rain during the night."

"There goes my fishing trip," Casey murmured. She tapped

the desk lightly with her knuckle. "I'm Detective O'Connor with Special Victims. Any chance I can chat with Marissa Goddard?"

"Oh, I'm sorry. She's at the courthouse. They're having a press conference." She glanced at her watch. "Right now, in fact. And finally, we can let Father Michael rest in peace. This whole thing has just been awful."

"Yes. Awful for a lot of people." Casey cleared her throat. "I'll just catch up with her at her hotel then. She's still at the Regency, right?" she asked casually.

"Oh, no. She's staying at the new Bentley Suites. I hear they're so luxurious."

"Bentley, that's right." Casey handed over one of her cards. "If she happens to come back here, let her know I'm looking for her."

"Of course, but she didn't act like she was coming back." The receptionist smiled. "In fact, she mentioned something about getting a bottle of Scotch and ordering pizza in."

"Nice way to unwind." Casey chuckled. "Thanks for your time. Try to stay warm now."

But the smile left her face as soon as she stepped back into the cold. It was too goddamn late to try to talk some sense into Marissa. She shook her head. Not that it would do any good. She pulled out her cell, dialing Tori as she hurried down the sidewalk to her car. She was surprised when she got voice mail.

"Hunter, it's me. I tried to catch Marissa at the church. No luck." She paused. "I thought maybe we could stop this damn press conference." She looked to the sky. "Well, I guess that's that. And in case you haven't heard, we're going to freeze our asses off tomorrow."

She slipped her phone back into her jacket pocket, then unlocked her car from twenty paces away and made a dash for it.

"Jesus," she muttered when she slammed her door, still shivering from the cold. She sat with the heater on high for a few moments, trying to decide what to do. An idea came to her, and she grinned wickedly as she drove away.

An hour and a half later, after Casey had talked the manager into letting her into Marissa's suite, she placed the pizza on the small bar along with the bottle of Scotch she'd picked up. She sat in one of the comfortable chairs in the sitting area. She didn't have to wait long.

"Ms. Goddard, good to see you again," she said evenly when the door opened. She was surprised at the composure Marissa maintained at finding her there.

"What the hell are you doing here, O'Connor? Breaking and entering?"

Casey pointed to the bar. "I brought you pizza."

"And Scotch? I see you've done your research."

Casey stood and leaned casually against the bar. "How did it go?"

"How did what go?"

"You know damn well what I'm talking about."

"It went lovely, O'Connor. Just lovely." She tossed her keys on the desk, along with her laptop. "In fact, it went so smoothly, I think the media here has lost interest in the case. There were hardly any questions."

"Well, you drag anything out long enough, there's always some new crisis to take its place. But no questions about Alice Hagen? I'm astounded."

"There was one mention of her, actually. And your chief called it a terrible coincidence after what had just happened to Father Michael." She smiled. "But I hear Homicide is on top of it."

"Oh, yeah. The evidence is just piling up," Casey said sarcastically. "And how do you sleep nights?"

"I sleep perfectly well, thank you." She opened the bottle of Scotch and filled two tumblers. "I'm just doing my job,

O'Connor." She slid one glass across the bar toward Casey. "In fact, my job is done. I've got some paperwork to complete tomorrow, then I'm out of here."

"That's quick. Hit and run, huh?"

Marissa laughed. "My flight isn't until Sunday night. Hit and run would get me out by noon tomorrow." She took a generous swallow of the Scotch and closed her eyes. "Nice," she murmured.

Casey swirled the amber liquid around before taking a sip. She nodded. Smooth. She drank the rest of it before sliding the glass back down the bar toward Marissa. "This is goddamn wrong and you know it."

"What I know or don't know is of no concern to you, O'Connor." She refilled both glasses. "I'm paid to make problems go away." She smiled as she slid the glass back to Casey. "Which was easy in this case, seeing as how both the mayor and the chief were willing to push the limits on what they controlled." She drank again. "Amazing, really."

Casey took another swallow, this one smaller as she looked at Marissa over the rim of the glass. "Fucking amazing," she said softly. "But what is everyone hiding, I wonder."

"Hiding?"

Casey lowered her glass. "Yes, hiding. The church is hiding something. The mayor is hiding something. The chief is hiding something. *You're* hiding something."

"Me? I assure you, I have nothing to hide."

"Really? Then perhaps you're just collectively hiding what everyone else is." She drained the rest of her Scotch. "Because you know all the secrets, don't you?"

"I know secrets, yes. But I hardly know all the secrets, O'Connor. After all, I'm still alive." She held the bottle out and Casey nodded.

"You know who the thirteenth print belongs to," Casey stated.

"Possibly."

"Which means you know who his lover was."

"Alleged lover," Marissa said as if on autopilot. She shoved the glass across the bar. "And before we get into another argument over it, no, I will not tell you. Because it matters not with this case."

Casey shook her head. "For the life of me, I can't understand why you care so little. These are people, human beings. Don't their deaths mean anything to you?"

"Oh, don't get all dramatic on me, O'Connor. Like I said, I'm just doing my job. And I'm very good at my job."

"It's a dirty, lonely job, though, isn't it?" Casey asked. "How do you cope?"

Marissa slipped off her suit jacket and tossed it on the chair. "I cope with Scotch," she said as she pointed at the rapidly emptying bottle. "And sometimes sex with a stranger does the trick too."

"Unfulfilling sex can't possibly ease your conscience." Casey pushed away from the bar and went toward her. "But I'm not really a stranger, am I?"

"I told you I wasn't going to sleep with you."

Casey smiled. "But you've changed your mind." She arched an eyebrow. "Haven't you?"

Marissa walked closer, her high heels making her taller than Casey. But it was the fire in her eyes that intimidated Casey, not her height. She ran her hand inside Casey's jacket, along her waist to her breast.

"Yes, I've changed my mind."

Before Casey could respond, Marissa had her pinned against the wall, both hands boldly cupping Casey's breasts.

"I don't plan to be gentle," Marissa murmured as her lips claimed Casey's.

Removing Marissa's hands from her breasts, Casey grasped Marissa's wrists, twisting them behind her back. "Neither do I," she countered as she spun her around, holding Marissa against the wall, and pressed her thigh between her legs. She heard Marissa gasp, saw her eyes flutter closed as her mouth parted. Casey's kiss was nearly bruising—or so she hoped—and when she released Marissa's hands, she felt Marissa's mouth still open to her. She shoved at Casey's jacket, sliding it down over her shoulders.

Casey had known her less than a week, had decided she didn't even like the woman, but she was as aroused as she could ever remember being. Her hands slid across the silk blouse, the smooth material cool to her touch. Without another thought, she ripped the tiny buttons off as she yanked the blouse apart, exposing the black lacy bra covering Marissa's full breasts.

Marissa moaned into her mouth, her hips pounding hard against Casey as she rode her thigh. Casey swore she could feel the wetness against her jeans and she leaned into Marissa, grinding hard against her.

"God, yes," Marissa murmured as she grasped Casey's shoulders, holding her tight.

Casey reached down, finding her way under Marissa's skirt. Frantically, she ripped at the sheer pantyhose blocking her. Desperate to be inside her, she pulled the offending hose away, her hand sliding smoothly into her wetness, her fingers impaling Marissa as she thrust into her.

"Yes, harder." Marissa gasped as she met each thrust of Casey's fingers. "*Harder*," she hissed.

Casey felt the perspiration on her brow as she held Marissa against the wall, her hand pumping faster and faster, the slick wetness dripping from her fingers. Marissa was panting, her hips rocking faster, each thrust harder than the one before, and Casey held on, her breathing matching Marissa's as she brought her to orgasm.

She squeezed her eyes shut as Marissa bit down hard against her neck, her body convulsing in Casey's arms as her climax hit, her scream muffled against Casey's throat.

"Jesus, O'Connor," she murmured between breaths. "That was a two-hundred-dollar blouse you just ripped."

Casey smiled stupidly as she tried to catch her breath, her fingers slipping from between Marissa's legs, moving against her waist, painting Marissa's skin with her own wetness. She felt Marissa's fingers caress her face and she opened her eyes, surprised at the warmth in the blue eyes that looked back at her.

"If you don't have anywhere to be this afternoon, I'd like for you to stay."

Casey nodded, glancing from Marissa's eyes to her lips, then back again. "Okay, yeah."

Marissa smiled. "Good." She leaned closer, her lips moving lightly against Casey's. "But this doesn't change anything, O'Connor. I'm still not telling you any secrets," she whispered.

"I never thought you would. *Oh.*" She gasped as Marissa's hand pressed between her legs. Casey could feel how damp her jeans were, proving the extent of her arousal.

Marissa tilted her head back, their eyes meeting. "You're very wet, Detective."

"*Yes,*" Casey breathed as Marissa's hand continued to move against her.

"For some reason, I thought this was a game to you."

"No game," Casey murmured. She took Marissa's hand and slipped it inside her jeans, her eyes closing as Marissa's fingers pushed into her wetness. "Very real."

CHAPTER TWENTY-THREE

Casey opened her eyes, surprised at the darkness in the room. She shifted, smiling as Marissa quietly protested the movement. Her hand slipped from Casey's breast, resting lightly at her waist. It felt good.

"What time is it?" Marissa murmured sleepily.

"After six."

"Damn, O'Connor . . . *six*?"

She rolled away from Casey, pulling the covers with her, leaving Casey exposed, naked, as she went across the room, turning on a lamp to chase the shadows away.

Casey sat up, reaching for her shirt and sweater, then stopped as Marissa chuckled.

"You're shy?" she asked. "After what we just did, I wouldn't think you'd be shy." She came back to the bed, tossing Casey the sheet. "There. I'd rather have you naked."

"I'm not sure I have the energy to be naked any longer," Casey said with a laugh.

"Sadly, I have to agree with you." She crawled back in bed, sliding closer to Casey. "It was fantastic, by the way."

Casey grinned. "Yeah, it was, wasn't it?"

Marissa laughed. "That wasn't a compliment meant solely for you. I think I did participate, you know. But it was a great way to spend the afternoon."

Casey rolled to her side, facing Marissa, unable to get the silly grin off her face. Hunter would kill her, of course. She was sleeping with the enemy, after all. But none of that mattered right now. She was tired, both mentally and physically, and so she closed her eyes as her hand snaked along Marissa's thigh, pausing when she reached the curve of her hip. She was disappointed when Marissa halted her motions.

"O'Connor, we need to talk," she said.

Casey opened her eyes. "Now?"

"I know who the thirteenth print belongs to."

Casey propped herself up on her elbow, but she said nothing.

"Father Tim—Timothy Resson—was transferred out of here four days before the murder," she said.

"Why do you think he was the one?"

"I . . . I got into Monsignor Bernard's personal files." Marissa sat up, leaning against the headboard, her gaze moving around the room nervously. "And I shouldn't be telling you any of this. I shouldn't have looked in the goddamn files to begin with." She took a deep breath. "I get paid to fabricate the truth, to exaggerate, to lie." She glanced quickly at Casey. "I hardly know what the truth is anymore."

"Then why are you telling me this?"

"Because you said I didn't care. The other day, you said I didn't care. Truth is, I do care. I care that a priest was murdered. I care that a nice grandmother was killed," Marissa said, her tone emphatic. "I'm not supposed to care, O'Connor. Like I said

156

before, it's not my job to care."

"Okay. I understand. You don't have to tell me anything. Just because we slept together—"

"This has nothing to do with the fact that we had sex, O'Connor." She closed her eyes. "Okay, maybe it does." She opened them again, turning to Casey. "Father Tim was transferred without cause, without notice. I found that in the regular files when I was going over the list of names submitted to you for prints. It piqued my curiosity. If there's one thing I learned from working with the churches in Boston, it's that there are always two files. One fit for the public . . . and one not."

Casey nodded. "Go on."

"Normally, if a priest is being transferred to another diocese or another parish, there's a paper trail of some sort, whether it's requesting housing arrangements, assignments, whatever. To make the arrangements for a transfer, it usually takes months, not days." She twisted the sheet nervously between her hands. "Monsignor Bernard's files were much more revealing. He knew they were having an affair. He blamed Father Michael, but because of his standing at the church, he couldn't transfer him without it raising questions. So, he sent Father Tim away. Sent him out West somewhere. Balmorhea?"

"Yeah. It's a little town out in West Texas, near the Davis Mountains." Casey knew the area. "It's in the middle of nowhere."

"Apparently that's where you go when you're being punished."

"So, Monsignor Bernard initiated the transfer?"

"It appears that way on paper. Of course, the bishop would have to sign off on it." She shrugged. "A normal transfer, it's just a formality to have the bishop approve it. In this case, I would assume Monsignor Bernard revealed the reason to Bishop Lewis. Especially in light of the fact that this particular diocese had taken some heat in the past for trying to cover up sex abuse accusations, I'm certain the bishop knew. Unless, of course, Monsignor Bernard thought he could handle it on his own, which is how these things escalate into cover-ups."

Casey sat up, ignoring the sheet that slipped to her waist. "I've not met him, but do you think Monsignor Bernard is capable of murder?"

Marissa laughed. "Oh, please. Bernard? No way. Despite his size—he's probably eighty to a hundred pounds overweight—he comes across as very mild-mannered. Weak, even."

"Just because someone is mild-mannered doesn't mean he's not capable of killing. But if he's a large man, he's probably not exactly light on his feet. Hidalgo's killer—and Alice Hagen's for that matter—slipped in and out without being seen or heard."

"I've read the reports. Hidalgo lived on the third floor. I'm not sure the monsignor could have made it up three flights of stairs without suffering a heart attack. He gets winded just walking down the hall." She shook her head. "He's not your killer."

Casey got out of bed, searching the floor for her clothes. "I hope you don't view this as a hit and run," she said with a smile as she held up her jeans. "But I think I need to interview this Father Tim person."

"O'Connor, what I just told you is off the record, you understand that, right?"

"Of course."

"So if Father Tim gives you anything useful, you can't really use it. Because technically you don't know he exists."

"If Father Tim got transferred four days before the murder, I doubt he's going to know anything. But he might help us to learn the why of it all. Why was Father Michael killed by Juan Hidalgo? Maybe there was a grudge between them that Father Tim knows about." She pulled her sweater over her head. "Or maybe it's like you said all along, just a murder without a cause."

"You don't believe that any more than I do."

Casey grinned. "No, I don't." She sat back down on the bed.

"Thank you."

"For sex?"

Blushing, Casey laughed. "No, for telling me what you knew. Because I didn't want to believe that you didn't care."

"I've made a living out of not caring, O'Connor. This case just struck a nerve, is all. It has nothing to do with you."

"You could have lied and said it had everything to do with me," she said as she leaned closer. "Thanks for the afternoon. It's one I won't soon forget," she murmured before she kissed her.

Marissa grabbed her arm as Casey stood to go. "My flight is Sunday evening." Their eyes met. "If you'd like to . . . well, if you want to get together, call me."

"Absolutely." Casey headed to the door, then looked back at her. "Yeah, absolutely."

CHAPTER TWENTY-FOUR

"Come on, Hunter, open up," Casey yelled as she pounded on the door. "It's freezing out here." She shivered as she looked up into the dark sky, wondering when the freezing rain would start.

Tori opened the door, standing there in a pair of gray sweats and bare feet, a beer bottle held casually in one hand. She smiled slightly, then motioned for Casey to go inside. "So, O'Connor, you get lost this afternoon or what?"

Casey hoped Tori couldn't see the blush that crept up her face, but she laughed. "Yeah, Hunter, lost. Lost for hours." She slipped off her jacket and tossed it across a chair, then reached for a slice of the pizza Tori had set out on the coffee table. She never did get to eat pizza with Marissa. "It was fabulous, by the way."

"Please say you didn't."

"Oh, but I did." She pointed at the beer. "Got another?"

"Yeah, I got another, but what the hell are you doing here? You don't have to give me a play-by-play of your afternoon, you know," she said, going to the fridge. She pulled out two bottles and handed one to Casey.

"As if I could. But we're gonna have to cancel our fishing plans for tomorrow." She twisted the cap off and tossed it to Tori.

Tori raised her eyebrows. "I thought even sex wasn't enough to make you miss a fishing date," she chided her.

"Not sex. And not even the cold weather. You need to pack a bag." She stepped out of the kitchen and looked down the dark hallway. "Where's your bedroom?"

"Pack a bag for what?"

"We're going to Balmorhea. To interview the thirteenth print." She grinned. "She gave up the name."

"My, you *are* persuasive."

"She said it had nothing to do with me."

"Right. And she told you the name before or after you slept together?"

"Could have been after, Hunter." She grabbed Tori's arm. "Come on, pack a bag."

"Road trip?"

"Oh, hell, no. We've got a flight to Midland. From there, we're renting a car and driving to Balmorhea. And let me tell you, renting a car in Midland ain't exactly easy."

"West Texas? Are you sure about this, O'Connor?"

"Of course I'm sure. It's another priest." Casey glanced at her watch. "Now, hurry up. Our flight's at nine."

"How did you manage tickets so quick?"

"I called your Lieutenant Malone. It's not a commercial flight."

Tori flipped on the light in the bedroom, staring at her. "*My* lieutenant?"

161

"Yeah. He called in a favor. He also said I'm to keep you on a tight leash and to not let you do anything stupid."

"Me? I'm not the one suggesting we fly out to goddamn West Texas to interview a priest about a case that's now closed." She turned around. "Closed, O'Connor. For real. So why in the hell did Malone agree to this?"

"We're not working on Father Michael's case, Hunter. I know it's closed. You have an open case on Hidalgo, right? Maybe Father Tim knows something."

Tori narrowed her eyes. "You working for Homicide now, O'Connor?"

Casey laughed. "Damn, Hunter, if I didn't know you were really a big softie, I might be intimidated by that scowl." She noticed a framed picture on the dresser and picked it up. "That Sam?"

"Yeah. That was out at the boat last summer."

"She's a beauty." Casey admired the photo of the two of them. "I was talking about the boat, of course." She put the picture back, her eyes still lingering on the photo of Sam with her arms around Tori's shoulders. "She's a knockout." She met Tori's eyes. "True love?"

Tori reddened but didn't look away. "Yeah."

Casey nodded. "Good. Glad to know it's out there. Because someday I'm going to have that too."

"And in the meantime?"

"In the meantime, there's nothing wrong with spending an afternoon with Marissa Goddard having fabulous sex." She grinned. "She's got stamina, I'll say that." She pointed to the large backpack Tori held. "Pack it. Oh, and did I mention it was snowing out there?"

CHAPTER TWENTY-FIVE

"If this trip turns out to be bullshit, I may never speak to you again," Tori hissed as they hurried across the tarmac.

Casey followed, the cold, biting wind hitting her in the face. "At least it's not snowing anymore."

"Small comfort, considering it's in the fucking teens with gale-force winds."

Casey laughed but the wind carried it away. And she had to agree with Hunter. Snowing or not, it felt as if they'd flown to the Arctic, not the high desert of West Texas.

"This is the airport, right?" Tori asked as they stood at the unmarked double doors leading into a low-slung building.

"I hope so, seeing as how the plane landed here and all." They'd been the only passengers on the flight. She opened the door, then motioned for Tori to precede her. "Age before beauty."

Tori rolled her eyes. "You're such a kid."

"But a cute kid." Casey stopped as the doors closed behind them, feeling every eye in the place on them. Of course, there were only four other people inside, so it was most likely true.

"You *sure* this is an airport?" Tori murmured.

Undeterred, Casey nudged her arm. "Come on." She smiled broadly at the woman behind the counter. "How's it going?"

"Wonderful. Yours was the last flight tonight." She waved across the room to one of the crew leaving. "See you tomorrow, Hank."

"Great. Last flight." Casey winked at Tori. "Told you it was the airport."

"Unlike those big-city places, we actually shut down at night. Which is what I'm about to do."

"Wonderful. Well, we won't keep you." Casey tapped the counter. "We're from out of town. I've arranged for a rental car. Do you know where we pick those up?"

"Rental car? The only place that rents cars is the Ford dealership in town. Is that what you mean?"

Casey sighed. "Not sure. The arrangements were made for me." She opened her phone, her thumb moving quickly as she searched through her numbers, finally finding it.

"They open up at seven," the woman told Tori.

"That's lovely," Tori said dryly. She leaned closer. "Maybe we should call the local police or sheriff," she suggested.

Casey glanced up, listening to their exchange.

The woman's eyes widened. "What for?"

"I'm Detective Hunter and the whiz kid here is Detective O'Connor, from Dallas. And if we don't have a rental car, I'm going to hope that your local police department will help us out." She drummed her fingers impatiently on the counter. "So, you want to call them or what?"

"*You're* the police?"

"Detectives," Tori corrected.

164

"I wasn't expecting . . . women," she said with a slight hint of distaste.

Just then, Casey's contact picked up and she confirmed the details of the car rental. "Supposed to have a car here waiting." She looked closer at the woman's nametag. "Dorothy. Supposed to have a car here."

"Yes. As I was telling her, I was expecting men." She bent down and came back up with a set of keys. "They delivered a car a couple of hours ago. It's an SUV, what with the weather and all." She handed the keys to Casey. "Sorry about that."

"Not a problem," Casey said as she pocketed the keys. "We've got reservations. Holiday Inn?"

"Yes, it's down on the interstate. Head back toward town, you can't miss it."

"They got a bar there? A restaurant?"

Dorothy glanced at her watch. "At *this* hour?"

Tori looked at Casey and leaned closer. "I hate you," she whispered.

"Nothing like sitting in a hotel bar in Midland, Texas, on a Friday night," Casey said as she held up her drink. "Cheers."

Tori flicked her glance to the three other patrons in the bar, all sitting on barstools watching a late basketball game on ESPN. She nodded as she tipped her own drink in Casey's direction. "I'm still trying to figure out how you talked me into this trip to begin with. I mean, one minute, I'm sitting at home enjoying beer and pizza for dinner and the next, I'm sitting in a Holiday Inn bar in the middle of nowhere."

Casey leaned closer. "Aren't you just dying to talk to him?"

Ah, Father Tim. Tori took a sip of her margarita. "I see you're still rather proud of yourself."

"The elusive name of the lover. Yeah." Casey took a large swallow from her drink. "Pretty good," she said. "Not a Rios

Rita, but pretty good."

"A margarita expert? I figured you for beer."

"Beer's for fishing." Casey grinned. "And pizza." She spun the paper coaster around on the table. "Tell me about Sam," she said unexpectedly.

"What about her?"

"What's she like? Tell me about you two."

Tori smiled as she thought of Sam. "I miss her."

"Yeah, well, you're stuck with me. So, what's she like?"

"She's . . . she's gentle. She's soft where I'm hard. She's compassionate. People like her." Tori shrugged. It was true. "Which is why we worked well together. People don't generally like me."

"You know, I asked around about you. I heard horror stories." Casey laughed. "But I like you. What does that say about me?"

"I don't normally open up to people," Tori admitted, oddly not uncomfortable with the conversation. "I don't really have friends."

Casey raised her eyebrows. "Just Sam?"

"We like being together. And Sikes, well, he's become a pal. He likes to fish so he comes out to the boat some." She nodded at Casey. "I'm going to guess you've got lots of friends."

Casey smiled sadly. "Lots of friends, yeah. Lots of acquaintances." She sipped her margarita. "Just not that one person, you know."

"Yeah, I know. There was never anybody for me. Sam came into my life and didn't give me a chance to run."

"You tried?"

"Oh, yeah. I was scared to death." She met Casey's eyes. "Still am."

"I miss not having somebody at home. After a bad day, I miss not having someone to talk to."

"If you miss it, then you must have had it."

"Oh, a few years ago I was with someone. I thought maybe she could be the one." Casey shook her head. "Didn't work out.

She couldn't understand the job. She wanted me to quit, to do something normal," she said with a laugh.

"Sam's boyfriend was the same."

Casey's eyes widened. "Boyfriend?"

Tori nodded. "Robert. Defense attorney."

"You dog. She was seeing a man when you met?"

"Yeah. But it's not like you think. We didn't start an affair or anything. She broke up with him. She knew he wasn't the one. With us, it just kinda happened. We had been dancing around it." Tori smiled. "Like I said, I didn't stand a chance."

"You ladies want another round?" the bartender called from across the bar.

"Absolutely." Casey held up her glass. "But at your age, you better not overdo it, Hunter. We've got a two-hour drive in the morning."

"I think I can keep up with your scrawny ass, O'Connor."

Casey laughed. "Yeah, I like you, Hunter. Good to see you've still got a sense of humor."

"What do you mean?"

"This job." Casey spun the coaster round and round on the table. "How do you do it? Death all the time."

Tori looked up at the TV, watching without interest, wondering at her answer. "Murder—death—it hit close to home when I was younger," she said quietly. It was still hard to talk about. Even with Sam, she didn't talk about it. She glanced over at Casey. "It was never solved. No one was ever brought to justice. I do it for them."

Casey frowned. "Who?"

Tori wasn't going to go there tonight. "I'll tell you about it as soon as you tell me about this brother you don't talk to."

Casey looked away. "It's nothing big, Hunter. It's nothing pretty, you know."

"Maybe you'll tell me someday. And maybe I'll tell you." She thanked the bartender who'd brought their fresh drinks. "But there is a lot of death, yeah. It's hard sometimes to remember there's more to life than this job."

"I guess so. Your victims are always dead."

"But how do you deal with the sexual assault—rape—all the time?"

Casey tipped her glass toward Tori. "You mean as opposed to murder? At least mine are alive. But it's the kids that are the worst. Man, I've seen some shit, Hunter. Some stuff you wouldn't believe." She met Tori's eyes. "Nightmare material. But my shrink says it's perfectly normal to have nightmares about it."

Surprised, Tori raised her eyebrows. "You see a shrink?"

"Well, she prefers to be called *therapist*, but yeah, at least once a month, whenever I need to talk. Don't you?"

"Oh, hell, no," Tori said. "It's just bullshit. I don't want someone psychoanalyzing me and poking around in my brain."

Casey laughed. "No, I don't suppose you do, Hunter. But I took a lot of classes in college. In fact, I thought I wanted to be a therapist myself. So I don't mind her poking around my brain."

They were quiet for a moment, both twisting their glasses on the bar. Finally, Tori tapped the table lightly, waiting until Casey looked at her. "So, you have nightmares?" she asked quietly.

"Yeah. Sometimes, yeah."

Tori thought about that for a moment, remembering her own nightmares. "What does she say about that?"

"She says when I stop having dreams about it all, that's when I'll know I've stopped caring."

Tori nodded again, but didn't say anything.

"You dream?" Casey asked, staring at her. "Nightmares?"

Tori nodded again. "Sometimes."

Casey reached out and quickly squeezed Tori's hand. "Good. I'd hate to think you didn't care anymore."

CHAPTER TWENTY-SIX

"You're kinda quiet this morning, Hunter."

At the sound of Casey's voice, Tori opened her eyes briefly. "I wonder why," she murmured. The tiny headache from earlier had turned into a throbbing monster.

Casey laughed. "That last margarita do you in?"

"Let me just say again, this trip better be worth it."

"Look at it this way, we've had some quality time together, not to mention this beautiful scenery we're getting this morning."

Tori looked out the window at the rocky, treeless landscape that sped by as Casey drove them south to Balmorhea. "Right. Just beautiful, O'Connor." She closed her eyes again. "Wake me when we're there."

"You don't want to talk? Visit?"

"No."

"You want to talk about fishing?"

"No."

"And you're sure you don't want me to tell you about my afternoon with Marissa?"

"Shut up before I shoot you," Tori murmured.

"Hey, Hunter, wake up."

Tori rolled her head toward Casey. She couldn't quite bear to open her eyes. "What?"

"We're here." Casey paused. "I think."

Tori cracked her eyes open and peered out the window. "You think?"

"It's not exactly a booming metropolis." Casey slowed at a blinking light before proceeding through the intersection. "In fact, it's smaller than I imagined."

Tori sat up and stretched, feeling a little better after her nap. She reached down for the bottle of water, drinking nearly half of it in one swallow.

"Yeah, tequila makes you thirsty."

Tori narrowed her eyes. "Shut up."

Casey laughed, pointing down a side street. "Downtown? Wow, it looks kinda like an Old West town."

She turned, driving them down the wide street, the area bustling with activity. Ranchers in town for the day, Tori thought. The old brick and stone buildings—some two stories, others with façades—still housed businesses, and most seemed to be doing a booming business on this cold Saturday morning.

"I guess Saturday is the day everyone comes into town for shopping," Casey commented. "What do you think people do for a living out here?"

"Ranching, most likely. Old homesteads have probably been in the family for generations."

"Yeah, but is there any grass or anything? It looks desolate."

"It's winter, O'Connor."

They passed through the two blocks of the old downtown area, coming upon what appeared to be a school. Beyond that, Tori spotted the telltale signs of a Catholic church. The ancient adobe building stood tall at the corner of town, and a massive wooden cross erected right by the road shadowed a small sign, *Our Lady of Guadalupe Catholic Church.*

"This is it," Casey said unnecessarily.

"It looks deserted."

Casey drove past the church, no doubt looking for an office or something. There were three buildings behind the church but all appeared to be closed and unoccupied. "Surely there's someone around. Churches don't close, do they?"

Seeing a narrow entry, Tori pointed. "Go through here."

"It looks like a private drive."

"Yeah. The rectory is probably back here."

"Good, Hunter. There's a car." Casey slowed, pulling to a stop beside it, its paint chipped and faded.

"That thing has seen better days."

"I'll say."

They both got out, their breath frosting around them as they headed to the door. The rectory was a modest building, painted white at one time. But it, like the car, was showing signs of wear and neglect. Tori stood by, hands shoved deep in the pockets of her jacket, while Casey went up the wooden steps and knocked on the door.

"So he doesn't know we're coming, right?" Tori said.

"No."

"And what are your plans if he's not here?"

"Where do you think he'd be, Hunter? Vacation?"

"Hell, I don't know. I just know it's cold, I have a headache, and you've dragged me out to the middle of nowhere to interview a man who had an affair with a dead priest on a case that's now closed," she stated, her voice rising with each word.

"Damn, you're cranky this morning."

Tori narrowed her eyes. "Knock again."

But before Casey could pound on the door, it opened.

"Good morning."

Casey and Tori exchanged glances as an elderly man greeted them.

Casey said, "Father Tim?"

He smiled. "No, no. He's at the church this morning. I'm Father Wayne. May I be of assistance?"

Casey shook her head. "Actually, we just wanted to have a word with Father Tim. Is it possible for us to just go on over?"

"Certainly. He's hearing confessions this morning." He raised his eyebrows. "Are you in need?"

"Not me, no." She gestured at Tori. "But my friend here is in dire need."

Embarrassed, Tori scowled. "Can we go now?"

"Thank you, Father Wayne. We'll just head on over to the church." Casey nodded, taking Tori by the arm and chuckling as they walked away.

"I would think after the afternoon you spent with Marissa, *you'd* be the one in need," Tori said as she jerked her arm away.

"You ever been to confession, Hunter?"

"I'm not Catholic. You been?"

"Yeah. When I was a kid."

"It never occurred to me you were Catholic." But with a name like O'Connor, she shouldn't be surprised.

"No, I'm not. Well, not anymore," she said. "Kinda goes along with . . . you know, that story about my brother."

They paused at the door to the church, both looking at it, then looking at each other.

"So, what, we just go on in?" Tori asked quietly, uncertain as to protocol.

Casey shrugged. "I guess."

"Want to tell me about your brother?"

"No."

Still shivering from the cold, Tori took her hands out of her pockets. "Want me to open the door?"

Casey laughed. "We're a pair, huh?"

Tori laughed too. "Yeah. It's just a building, right?"

"I suppose."

"So, you want me to open the door?"

"I guess one of us should."

Just then the door swung open and a young priest stood there, his own jacket collar standing up to guard against the wind. "Oh, you startled me," he said. "You're here for confession, I assume." He glanced at his watch. "I stop hearing confessions at ten. We have an early Mass today at noon. For the funeral, you know."

"Actually, we're not here for confession," Tori said. She pulled out her badge and held it up. "I'm Detective Hunter. This is Detective O'Connor. We're from Dallas."

His eyes widened and he looked away. "I see. I suppose you're here to talk about Michael."

"Yes. Is there someplace we can talk?" Casey asked.

"I share the rectory with Father Wayne. There'll be no privacy there." He pointed back to the church. "We can go inside."

Tori took a step back. "In the church?"

"Yes. The heat is on. It's warm inside."

"Is there no place else?" Casey asked.

He leaned closer. "I assure you, you'll be perfectly safe inside," he said quietly. "After all, I've survived it."

Casey laughed. "Yeah. I guess." She looked at Tori. "Okay?"

Tori let out a deep breath, then nodded. Sam would think she was being silly. In fact, she knew she was. She was an adult, not a child. But those long-ago memories, those few terrifying minutes at the church when the caskets were being closed—locking her family away forever—leaving her alone, those memories still haunted her.

Casey nudged her when Father Tim held the door open for them. "You okay?" she whispered.

Tori took another deep breath, looking into the concerned eyes of her new friend. Genuine concern, she noted. So she nodded and gave a half-smile. "Childhood memories."

"I completely understand."

Father Tim led them inside, and Tori walked shoulder-to-shoulder with Casey, glancing around the church quickly.

"Here," he said, pointing to the last row of pews. "We can sit back here."

"It's kinda dark in here," Tori murmured.

"Yes. We rely on the windows for most of our light. We're hoping the sun will break through by noon."

"What do you do at night?"

"We light the candles," he said, pointing to the candle sconces that adorned each of the large pillars lining the church.

Tori cleared her throat. "Well, first of all, let me say how sorry I am about Father Michael."

Father Tim nodded sadly. "I only found out three days ago. I still can't believe it." He shook his head. "They haven't really told me anything, just that he was found dead a few days after I left." He sighed. "You see, I'm being punished. I'm not really allowed contact with the outside. No TV, no phone, no papers."

Tori and Casey exchanged glances. "He was found strangled," Tori said quietly. "In the rectory."

Father Tim gasped, his face drawn in shock. "He was killed?" he whispered. "But no, they told me he was found dead, that Alice found him. They didn't say anything about foul play." He closed his eyes. "Who would do such a thing?"

"It was . . . it was Juan Hidalgo," Casey said.

His eyes widened. "No. Can't be. Juan would never do such a thing. Juan owed him so much." He shook his head. "No. Not Juan."

"What do you mean he owed him?" Tori asked.

174

Father Tim tilted his head back, staring at the ceiling. "A year or so ago, when Monsignor Bernard found out about Juan's legal troubles, he wanted to fire him. But Michael insisted he could be trusted, insisted Juan was a changed man. He fought for him. And Bernard finally gave in. Juan was so grateful. There's no way he would harm Michael. No way."

"We think he was coerced, or blackmailed perhaps, forced in some way by someone else."

"Well, surely he would tell you. Juan Hidalgo is no killer."

"Well, you see, Juan is also dead," Casey said. "He was killed the same day. Shot to death."

"Oh, no. No, no." He stood and walked into the aisle, turning to face the altar. "What has happened?" he asked quietly, his shoulders slumped. He turned back toward them. "Who?"

Tori raised both hands in a shrug. "We have no idea. We were hoping maybe you might be able to help us."

"Me?"

"Father Michael was obviously killed for a reason. We thought maybe it had something to do with your affair."

He turned back toward the altar. "I got sent away to end our affair, Detective Hunter. I can't imagine Michael was killed because of it."

"How did your leaving come about?" Casey asked.

"Bernard was waiting for me at the end of Mass one day. He told me I'd been transferred. He had all my things packed, a car waiting. I wasn't allowed to talk to anyone. They just led me to the car and whisked me away," he said somberly. "We drove straight through. Hours and hours of listening to Monsignor Bernard list all my sins and broken vows." He laughed humorlessly. "It was a prelude to Purgatory, I'm certain. And when I got here, Father Wayne was put in charge of me. He counsels me daily on my . . . my affliction."

"Did Juan know of your affair?"

He nodded. "Yes, he did. He walked in on us one day." He

waved his hand dismissively. "It was nothing, really. Just an embrace. But obviously one made between lovers, not friends."

"When was this?"

"Oh, months ago. Early summer, I think. He asked Michael about it a week or so later. Michael didn't see the point of lying, even though we were being so very careful. He felt if he lied to Juan, it would just make him that much more curious."

"And he was okay with it?"

"He never really said anything. But he changed after that."

"How so?"

"He was more polite, more talkative, more friendly, if you will. He started bringing me things where before he would only bring something for Michael. Fresh pastries that his mother baked, tamales, things like that."

"So it wasn't like he became aggressive or anything," Tori stated.

"No, no. Juan was never aggressive. Juan had a drug problem. A serious one. But he kicked it. That was one reason Michael fought to keep him on."

"Who else may have known of your affair? Alice Hagen?"

"Oh, of course. A saint of a woman, that one. Her husband has been ill for the last fifteen years, yet she carries on, waiting on him hand and foot, never complains. Michael of course knew her for much longer than I did, yet she took a liking to me. She covered for us on more than one occasion. I won't say she totally understood our love, but she never questioned it. I think maybe she could see it, you know. When we were alone, we allowed ourselves to drop that shield, so I think she could see how deeply we cared for each other." He wrapped his arms around himself as he stared at the altar. "We were truly in love," he said. "We talked about leaving the Church." His shoulders sagged. "But what would we do? It was all either of us knew."

"There are other denominations that are accepting," Casey said after a quick glance at Tori.

He turned back toward them. "When I took my vows, I did so sincerely. I just didn't count on falling in love." He came closer and sat down in the pew again. "I had resolved myself that we had to be apart. At least for now. I have a hard time accepting that he's really gone. And I have a hard time accepting that Bernard didn't let me know, did not allow me to attend his funeral, especially after knowing how close we were."

"How do you think he found out?"

"I can't begin to know. We were careful. And Alice and Juan would never say anything. They were both loyal to us, Alice almost to a fault. Besides, she and Bernard never saw eye-to-eye. They bickered constantly. I can't imagine she would confide in him."

"When you say you were careful, how were you able to be together without anyone suspecting?"

He frowned. "Well, we lived together, shared the rectory."

Tori's jaw dropped. "Wait a minute. You lived there? No one ever made mention that you lived there. Not Monsignor Bernard, not Alice Hagen. In fact, I asked Mrs. Hagen point-blank if anyone else lived there and she said no."

"She was trying to protect our relationship. Bernard most likely was trying to avoid a scandal."

"How long did you live there?"

"Two years. But there was a third priest there for a while, Father Roberto—or Father Bob, as most called him. He was sent to another diocese in Arizona."

"Did he know of your affair?"

"No. He had actually moved on when our relationship began."

"Why wasn't another priest moved in?"

"Bernard likes to think of living at the rectory as a privilege. He hadn't yet decided who to reward, so we were alone for seven months."

"And you don't think he ever suspected?"

Father Tim shook his head. "No. Had he suspected, I would have been transferred out long before now."

Tori stopped her questions, and they were silent for a moment looking at each other.

Then Casey reached down the pew, gently touching Father Tim's arm. "I'm really sorry about your loss," she said. "I'm sorry you didn't have the chance to see him again. Because in the end, we're all just human, right?"

"Thank you. I'm really at a loss right now. I haven't been allowed to grieve, haven't been given the chance to reconcile my feelings. To know that his death was intentional makes it all the more difficult. It makes me regret so many things."

"Your relationship?"

"Oh, no. I regret not being strong enough to leave. I regret not standing up to Bernard and demanding that I be able to see Michael before I left. But really, I regret that Michael and I didn't just pack up and leave. I don't know what we were waiting on. It wasn't like anything was going to change, not for us. We'd hoped with the new Pope that perhaps some things would change, celibacy for one. With the shortage of priests, something has to give. But for us, no. Not in my lifetime. Much like you must feel, thinking you'll never see the day when you can freely marry."

Casey laughed nervously. "What? Are we wearing signs or something?"

Father Tim smiled gently. "I've counseled my share of homosexuals, Detective."

"And what do you tell them? That it's not too late to change?"

He shook his head. "There are enough hypocrites hiding behind God's cloak. I refuse to be one more. We all have our own relationship with God, talk to Him in our own way. Love is a gift from God. Do we deny that gift because man says it should not be so?"

"What will you do now?" Tori asked.

"I'm not sure. I always felt this was what I was called to do. I'm just not sure I can continue to do it with these restrictions. I think that, surely, God means for us to be true to ourselves." He looked again to the altar, his eyes thoughtful. "I loved Michael. We could have made a good life."

Tori and Casey exchanged glances, then Casey stood, gently touching his shoulder.

"We should go." She looked again at Tori. "If you're back in Dallas and need a friendly face, give me a call."

He took the card she held out, nodding slightly.

"Thanks for the information, Father," Tori said. "You've been very helpful."

"I guess I should thank you for filling in the blanks about Michael. Will you need me to testify to anything? I mean in court?"

Tori shook her head. "I don't think so. It shouldn't come to that."

"Very well." He stood. "As I said earlier, we have a funeral to prepare for. I suspect we shall have visitors very soon."

"Then we'll get out of your hair." Tori shook his hand, surprised at the firmness of his grasp. "Take care of yourself."

"Perhaps we'll meet again, Detective."

They left him still staring at the altar, no doubt deep in thought. Once the doors to the church shut behind them, they both turned up the collars on their coats to shield against the wind.

"That wasn't all that much fun," Casey said.

"Not too much, no."

They headed back along the sidewalk to their rental, both stopping when they reached it to look back at the church. Father Tim stood on the steps and raised a hand in their direction in farewell.

"He's a nice guy," Casey said. "And he's so totally alone."

179

Tori sighed but didn't comment.

"You didn't tell him about Alice Hagen. Why?"

Tori shrugged. "I didn't see the point. We'd already laid enough on him."

"He probably would want to know. You know, to contact the family or something."

Tori met her eyes. "You want to go tell him?"

Casey shook her head. "No. Let's get out of here."

CHAPTER TWENTY-SEVEN

Even though they'd talked it to death, Casey still wasn't satisfied with the outcome. She ignored Tori's heavy sigh as they exited the plane. "I'm just saying we should talk to him. What would it hurt?"

"On what grounds, O'Connor? And come on, do you really think Monsignor Bernard is capable of murder?"

"Like I said, I've never met the man, but I think all people are capable of murder, given the right circumstances."

Tori sighed again. "You've read the report on Hidalgo. The killer was in and out before anyone saw him. Bernard is a large man. No way he slipped up and down three flights of stairs unseen. And frankly, I'm not sure he could make it up three flights of stairs."

"But it makes sense. There was no breaking and entering. Same with Alice Hagen. They both knew their killer."

"Look, I'm not going to my lieutenant with this, O'Connor. He'll tell you what I'm telling you. We have no physical evidence. Not unless they've turned up something at the Hagens' residence since we've been gone."

They bypassed the crowd waiting at the baggage carousel, both walking with their backpacks slung over one shoulder.

"One advantage of flying small," Casey said, motioning around them. "Love Field beats the hell out of DFW."

"I hate flying."

Casey laughed. "Is that why you had a death grip on my hand during takeoff?"

Tori scowled. "I did not have a death grip." She peered around suspiciously. "And there's no reason to repeat that to anyone."

They walked out into the early evening, the temperature some forty degrees warmer than when they'd left Midland.

"Now this is what March is supposed to feel like. I hate winter."

Tori nodded. "It's almost fishing weather."

Casey scanned the parking lot. "Where the hell did I park?"

Tori pulled out her cell. "I'm going to give Sikes a call."

"Yeah, yeah. I'm more worried about my car. Why didn't we write it down?"

Tori followed Casey through the parking lot, the phone to her ear, then said, "Sikes, it's me. We're back. Got a few answers. Just wanted to see if you've got lab reports back on Alice Hagen. Give me a call."

Casey turned a circle, looking for her car. "I'm going to have to call goddamn security. I don't have a clue as to where we parked."

"Why don't you try setting off your alarm or something?"

"Now that's an idea, Hunter. I like that." Casey pulled her keys out, holding them high above her head as she walked along the rows, pushing frantically at the panic button. Finally, some ten minutes later, she heard the unmistakable sound of a car alarm. Two rows over—right under the light pillar with Section D painted prominently on the side—sat her car, lights flashing and horn honking. She laughed. "Yeah. Section D. I remember now."

"Turn that damn thing off."

She did. Then they walked through the lot, stopping at the trunk, where they both tossed in their packs. "So, you want to get dinner or something?"

Tori shook her head. "I'm beat. I think I'm just going to head on home."

Casey nodded. "Yeah, me too. I should probably do laundry. I'm fairly certain these are my last pair of clean jeans," she said, pointing at her legs.

"Well, let's get together tomorrow. If Sikes didn't get anything from the lab, we can at least go over what we got." Tori shrugged. "Maybe go out to the boat later if the weather holds."

"Yeah. Yeah, I'd like that." She slammed the trunk closed and looked up at the now dark sky. "Stars are out. Might have sunshine tomorrow."

Tori followed her gaze skyward, her mind not on fishing. She hadn't talked to Sam in two days. They'd done nothing more than exchange voice mails. She sighed, then looked at Casey. "Might have sunshine, yeah."

CHAPTER TWENTY-EIGHT

Casey reached for her coffee through her car window. "Thanks. Oh, and extra ketchup with those hash browns this time." She tore open the sugar packets, emptying the contents of both into the steaming coffee before taking a sip. She grimaced, then poured in a third sugar.

"Here you go, hon."

"Thanks, Dora," Casey said as she reached for the bag. "The coffee's a little stout this morning, isn't it?"

"That's because it's past morning and it's been sitting for an hour."

"It's barely ten. And it's Sunday."

"Then shouldn't you be in church?"

Casey smiled. "Do you abuse all your customers this way?"

"Only the regulars. See you next week," she said as she closed the window in Casey's face.

Casey pulled out one of the fat breakfast burritos as she drove away, wondering why she didn't find a new place for Sunday breakfast. But one bite into the soft flour tortilla stuffed full of scrambled eggs and Mexican sausage reminded her why.

"God, that's so good," she murmured, barely swallowing before she took a bite of the nearly foot-long hash brown stick.

She juggled burrito, coffee and cell phone as she drove, trying to find Marissa's number. She was surprised when it went immediately to voice mail.

She shrugged. "So I'll drive over."

"And pick up breakfast on your way."

"Breakfast? Come on, Sikes, what do you want? A muffin or something?"

"No, I don't want a muffin, Hunter. Go by that little taco place Sam likes so much."

Tori smiled. Yeah, okay. She could do that. Because she'd finally talked to Sam last night, if only for a few minutes. But Sam missed her. Sam missed her a lot. Sam probably missed going for tacos in the morning too.

"Okay, Sikes. Two with everything, right?"

"Yeah. And make sure you get extra avocado this time."

"Anything else, princess?"

"Other than coffee, no."

Tori folded her phone before Sikes could think of anything else, but she had a smile on her face. She had gone to bed at the ungodly hour of nine p.m. only to be awakened by the phone and Sam's voice at midnight. It was ten in California and Sam had just finished a two-day training session out in the desert.

"I'm not sure how that's going to help me in Dallas, but it was kinda fun," she said. "We were in four teams. It was a little like war games, I guess."

"So, you're liking it okay then?" Tori asked.

"Other than I miss you like crazy, yeah." Her voice lowered. "I really do miss you, Tori. God, I miss you so much."

Tori closed her eyes, letting Sam's words sink in. "I miss you being here, Sam. I miss our life."

"I had no idea it would be this hard. I had no idea I could miss someone this much." There was a pause, then Sam said, "Do you know what I really miss the most, Tori?"

"No."

"I miss looking into your eyes."

Tori's breath caught and she swallowed, finally clearing her throat. "I love you, Sam. Please don't forget that. I love you."

She smiled now as she remembered Sam's sharp intake of breath, Sam's murmured words back to her. Yeah, she had no idea she could miss somebody this much either. So she pulled into the drive-thru with a smile on her face, thinking she might get Sikes one of those Mexican pastries as a treat. Since Ramirez was gone, they'd missed his mother's nearly daily supply.

Casey smiled at the hotel desk clerk—the same one she remembered from Friday—while she waited for the couple in front of her to finish their check-in.

"You're that detective, right?"

Casey nodded, hoping she wasn't too late to catch Marissa. "O'Connor. Is she in?"

"No, I'm sorry. She already checked out."

Casey's heart sank as she glanced at her watch. "I guess she must have changed her flight. I thought she wasn't leaving until later."

"Oh, no, I think her flight's still the same. She said she had some last-minute business at the church."

"Well, great. Maybe I can catch her there." She tapped the counter as she left. "Thanks a lot."

❧

Sikes ripped open the bag Tori handed him, bypassing the two burritos for the treat she'd added. He took a large bite, his eyes closing. "God, that's so good." Then he grinned. "Not as good as Mama Ramirez, of course. Thanks, Hunter."

"Sure." She handed over the cup of coffee and sat down at her desk, opening up her own bag. She quickly unwrapped her burrito and took a bite. "You got Mac's report?" she asked.

"Yeah." He wiped his mouth, then sipped from his coffee. "Not a whole lot. The place was clean. But Spencer found a smudge on Hagen's forearm. Wasn't able to get a print, but it's a possible transfer from the killer. She's got the analysis there, but it's some kind of lotion, I think."

Frowning, Tori took another bite. "Lotion?"

"I think so. But what did you guys find out?"

Tori put her burrito down, snatching a napkin from Sikes. "Father Tim said both Hidalgo and Alice Hagen knew about their affair. He also said both of them were loyal to Father Michael and wouldn't have told Bernard. But the monsignor knew and they basically shipped Father Tim out of here without notice. He wasn't allowed to talk to Michael at all. And four days later, Michael is dead."

"So you think the monsignor is involved?"

Tori picked up her burrito again, then thought for a moment before taking a bite. "He's involved somehow, yes. If neither Alice Hagen nor Juan Hidalgo told him, how did he find out about the affair? And when he did find out about it, why did he send Father Tim away as if he's a criminal and not Father Michael? And why not just confront them about it?"

"Of course, you're just assuming Hagen and Hidalgo didn't talk."

"Yeah. But neither were on good terms with the monsignor, so why would they go and tattle about the affair?"

"But you don't think he killed them, do you?"

Tori shook her head. "No. And I'm not saying that just because he's a priest. He's a large, overweight man who looks like he's a candidate for a heart attack at any moment. I can't see him pulling off a murder. Especially Juan Hidalgo."

"Why?"

"Third floor, no elevator."

"So?"

"So I can't see a guy his size making it up three flights of stairs and still have the physical capability to pull off a murder."

Sikes shrugged. "He didn't seem all that winded."

Tori frowned. "What are you talking about? When?"

"When Ramirez and I were there trying to get statements. After you guys left."

Tori's eyes widened. "He was there?"

"Yeah. He came to console the family. And he didn't seem winded at all."

Tori stood up and began pacing. "He's winded just walking. The first time we met him at the rectory, he was winded. Even in his office that day, just talking to him, he sounded winded." It didn't make sense. "Not possible he walks up three flights of stairs."

"Well, he did."

Tori spun around. "Wait a minute. Didn't you and Ramirez say Juan was the maintenance man at his apartment building?"

"Yeah. So?"

"So it stands to reason then that he'd have a master key to all the rooms." Tori kept pacing as John finished off his second burrito. "Where is Spencer's report on Alice Hagen?"

"She e-mailed me the full report," he said as he pulled up his mail. "I doubt her file's been updated yet."

"Find the part about the lotion smudge."

CHAPTER TWENTY-NINE

Casey walked into the offices behind the church, surprised to find them unlocked. Even more surprising was the empty chair at the receptionist's desk. She paused, listening, but there was no sound. She glanced at her watch, wondering what time the church service would be over. It was nearly eleven now. But she didn't want to wait, so she went down the wide hallway, looking at each closed door, hoping she remembered which one was Marissa's temporary office.

She found it easily. It was the only one open.

She stood in the doorway, looking inside. It appeared to be undisturbed, but Marissa's purse and laptop lay unopened on the desk. Casey looked back down the hallway, then stepped inside, her curiosity getting the better of her. She placed her hand on the laptop. It was cold with no sign that it had been turned on recently. Beside Marissa's purse was her cell phone. Casey picked and flipped it open. It was turned off.

No wonder it went to voice mail, she thought.

She tossed it back down, turning a slow circle in the office, wondering what to do. Marissa was obviously still here. Somewhere. And Casey wanted to see her before she left.

So she went in search of her. Loudly.

"Marissa?" she called, looking down the hallway in both directions. "Marissa? You around?"

Silence.

She cocked her head. "Is anyone around?" she called again. "Hello?"

It was eerily quiet and she walked to the end of the hallway, trying every door. All were locked. At the very end were two double doors. They opened into a small amphitheater, but it too was dark and empty. So she turned back, going down the hallway to the reception area and entering the hall on the other side of the building. Here, the doors were massive, all with etched wood carvings. Elegant. Prestigious. She supposed these were the offices of Bishop Lewis. Perhaps Monsignor Bernard had an office here as well. She tried each door, but they were all locked.

"Hello? Anybody around?" she called again. "Marissa?"

Still nothing. Just the strange quiet. An unnatural quiet.

"Creepy," she murmured.

Tori leaned over John's shoulder, reading through Spencer's report and trying to sort through the medical jargon.

"Here," John said, pointing.

"Okay. Partial print. Too smudged for detail." She kept reading. "Lavandula extract, vegetable emulsifying wax, almond oil, aloe vera, vegetable glycerin, sea algae," she said. "What the hell?"

"Lotion."

"Wheat germ oil? Titanium dioxide? How the hell does this

help us?"

"I asked Mac to have one of his people analyze it. Maybe we can get a brand or something."

"Scroll back up. Cause of death reads nearly identical to Juan Hidalgo's. Are they confirming?"

"With no physical evidence, how can they?"

Tori started pacing again, moving behind John, her mind racing.

"I have a hard time believing Monsignor Bernard could have killed these people, but I have a memory of him using lotion." She shrugged. "Of course, does that really mean anything? Lots of people use hand lotion."

John leaned back, his arms crossed behind his head. "A lotion smudge won't help us. And we have no leads on either case. Tell me how someone could walk into both residences in broad daylight and no one see a thing?"

"Perhaps it's just that no one *noticed*," she said. "What if it's someone who people are used to seeing there? What if it's a frequent visitor so no one took notice?"

"And no evidence of a break-in. Would have to be someone they knew."

"Like a priest," she said quietly.

Casey retraced her steps through the quiet hallway one more time, finally giving up on finding Marissa. So she stopped by her office, intending to leave her a note, although she felt a bit like a snoop as she opened the middle drawer looking for paper and a pen.

She scribbled out a note, leaving her cell number and a request for Marissa to call her before she left town. She tucked the note under Marissa's phone and quietly shut the door.

Walking back to the reception area, she heard it. The slamming of a door and the sound of muffled voices, then the unmistakable sound of a sharp, quick scream. A woman.

Then quiet again.

She turned around, raising her eyes to the ceiling. It had definitely come from upstairs, but whether it was the second floor or not, she had no way of knowing. With the building closed and quiet, it could have been the third floor. So she bypassed the elevators and eased open the door to the stairwell. It was dark, lit only by soft glowing bulbs at the landing.

She took a deep breath, then moved up the stairs, sliding along the wall, her eyes turned upward. She peered through the glass on the door at the second floor, but the hallway was dark, no sign of movement. She carefully cracked the door, listening. Again, nothing.

As she crept into the hallway, turning around slowly, there was nothing but the eerie silence of an empty building. She was about to call out Marissa's name when she heard movement above her.

"Third floor," she murmured, heading back to the stairwell.

Taking the steps two at a time, she paused at the landing, her hand on the door. She reached to her side, briefly touching her weapon, feeling somewhat comforted by the cool metal against her hand. She wasn't sure what she expected to find but she had no intention of going out with her weapon drawn. So she let her leather jacket fall closed as she opened the door to the third floor.

But it too was dark and quiet. Thankfully, the plush carpet muffled any sound of her boots. There were a handful of doors on each side of the hallway, so she went to the first one, leaning closer, listening. She sighed when she heard nothing, then moved to the next. She was nearly to the end of the hallway before she heard a low voice—a man's voice.

Casey raised her hand to knock and then stopped, thinking better of it. Instead, she reached for the doorknob, slowly turning.

It wouldn't budge.

"Figures," she whispered. Taking a deep breath, she raised her hand again, this time knocking loudly on the door. Only a moment passed before she heard the man's voice again.

"Who is it?"

"I'm looking for Marissa Goddard," she called through the closed door. She tilted her head, waiting for a response. "I'm a friend of hers."

She heard footsteps approach and, out of habit, she reached to her side, her hand grazing her weapon. But she had no time to react when the door was pulled open and a gun barrel stuck in her face.

"Whoa, now," she said, taking a step back.

"Do not move."

She stopped, her gaze moving past the hulk of a man to see Marissa sitting on a chair, a rope tied tightly around her waist. She looked back to the man's puffy red face, taking in the perspiration on his brow, his labored breathing. Thinking back to Hunter's description, this had to be Monsignor Bernard.

"I shall assume you are the police." The gun came closer, the barrel nearly touching her forehead. "I don't need to remind you that I know how to use this gun."

Oh, man, this can't be good, she thought, blinking several times as she tried to focus on the handgun that was now touching the bridge of her nose. "I'm Detective O'Connor. I kinda had a date with Marissa," she said calmly.

"Well, as you can see, she's tied up at the moment."

Casey smiled. "I see that. So I guess I should just leave you to it and I'll catch up with her later."

"I'm sorry, but I no longer have a sense of humor, Detective. You will come inside." He stepped back. "Please hold your hands above your head."

She did as she was told, watching him closely, looking for the opening she needed. But her eyes widened as the monsignor darted over to Marissa, belying his size, and he put the gun against her temple. Marissa's eyes were swimming in fear as she looked at Casey.

He said, "Please place your gun on the table beside you."

Casey tilted her head. "I don't think that's a good idea."

"Detective, I have no intention of hurting either one of you."

"Well, seeing as how you've got a gun pointed at her head, forgive me if I'm hesitant to believe you."

"Let me rephrase, Detective. I have no *intention* of hurting either one of you, but that doesn't mean I won't if you do not place your gun on the table," he said, his voice rising.

Casey could see the vein pounding rapidly in his head as his face reddened. She glanced at Marissa, meeting her frightened eyes. It went against all protocol to give up her weapon. But she also knew that if he was serious, nothing she tried would be quick enough to stop him.

"Okay," she said. "Okay." She slowly reached to her side, sliding her weapon out of the small leather holster she wore. "Take it easy." She didn't know if she was talking to him or to herself.

"Place it on the table. And your cell phone, please turn it off. Lay it on the table with the gun and move away."

She did as he asked, stepping away from the table as he moved behind Marissa, the gun still held to her head.

"Way to go, O'Connor," Marissa said, her voice shaky, hinting at her fear. "Maybe I should have slept with Hunter. I doubt she'd give up her weapon this easily."

Casey laughed nervously. "No. She also wouldn't have slept with you."

"Do you have handcuffs?" Monsignor Bernard asked.

"Oh, man, you're not going to make me use handcuffs, are you? That's so humiliating to use my own cuffs."

CHAPTER THIRTY

"Come on, Hunter. I think you're overreacting," Sikes said as he held on when she squealed around a corner, one hand on the wheel and the other dialing her cell. "Are you trying to kill us or what?" he hissed.

"I'm trying to get to the goddamn church."

"We can't go busting in on him. We don't have a warrant," he reminded her for the third time.

"She's not answering her phone. Marissa Goddard is not answering her phone. Something is going on."

"Ever think they might be together and turned their phones off?"

"Then I'm likely to kill her myself."

Her phone rang and she fumbled with it as she drove, glancing at Sikes.

"About time," she muttered, easing up on the accelerator.

"You better have a goddamn good excuse for not answering your phone, O'Connor."

"And hello to you too, Hunter." It was Mac.

Tori held the phone to her chest for a moment, her jaw clenched, before putting it back to her ear. "Mac, I'm sorry. I thought it would be O'Connor."

"Obviously. But Sikes said to give you a ring about the lotion. We narrowed it down to a brand, believe it or not. Don't know if it'll help you any. It's Organic Lavender Hand Cream. Peaceful Herbs Farm is the brand name. It's got French lavender and Roman chamomile. It's amazing what this new analysis can do for us, Hunter. We were able to pinpoint even trace ingredients, just from this smudge. Imagine how this can help—"

"Yeah, yeah, Mac, just imagine," she said, cutting him off. "Kinda in a hurry here, you know. You got anything else? We're about to go busting in at the church without a warrant."

"I'm assuming Malone doesn't know this?"

Tori grinned. "No. And Sikes has already pissed his pants." She jumped as John took a swipe at her. "Thanks for the info, Mac. We'll be in touch." She cut him off in mid-sentence as she folded her phone. "Try O'Connor again, Sikes. I'll try to keep two hands on the wheel this time."

"I don't know why the hell I listen to you. We're going to get busted big-time for going in without a warrant." He flipped open his phone. "I miss Ramirez. He never did this shit to me."

"Big baby."

"I'm serious, Hunter. When Malone tries to bust our ass, you're taking the heat for this, not me." He looked at his phone, letting out a sigh. "What's her number?"

"Pull a chair next to Ms. Goddard, please. Sit down, slip your arms between the bars and cuff your hands behind your back."

Casey did as she was told, briefly considering leaving one side unlocked, then thinking better of it as the monsignor moved behind them to watch her progress.

"There. All locked up," she said, pulling her arms out to her side to show him.

"It was a good choice you made, Detective O'Connor." He went over to the table where her weapon lay, then placed his own beside it. "As I said, I have no intention of harming you. I simply cannot live with what I've done any longer." He lifted the lid on a large box that sat on a leather sofa. "I have my confession to make. I had intended on Ms. Goddard being my witness. It appears you will be as well, Detective."

"Then why the gun? Why are we tied up?"

"I have killed two people. But I am not ready for the police to arrive."

Casey looked at Marissa with raised eyebrows.

Marissa gave a subtle shrug. "I have no idea," she whispered.

They watched in silence as he pulled a long, white linen robe from the box and slipped it on, struggling to secure it over his large belly. He leaned on the desk as he breathed heavily, then he stood straight and pulled a beautiful purple stole from the box and draped it over both shoulders. On top of this, he hung a wooden cross around his neck, the cross bouncing against his stomach as he turned back toward them.

With his hands raised skyward, he tilted his head back, looking to the ceiling. "Bless me, Father, for I have sinned. And sinned again." He lowered his head, the cross around his neck moving with each breath he took. "I killed Juan Hidalgo. And I killed Alice Hagen," he said in a low tone. "I was not strong enough to say no."

Puzzled, Casey watched him, her brow drawn tight. "Excuse me, but do we get to ask questions? Or what?"

He lifted his head, his eyes meeting Casey's. "You're not Catholic, are you? Not familiar with the confessional process?"

"Not so much, no."

"But you were raised Catholic, I'm guessing?"

Casey nodded. "My parents divorced when I was young. It was kinda nasty. My mother never went back to church after that. And then, well, I got older."

"Do you wish for confession then, Detective? I will hear it."

"Oh, hell, no. That's just a bunch of crap, as far as I'm concerned."

His lips pursed as he shook his head disapprovingly. He turned his back and went to look out a far window.

Marissa kicked her in the ankle. "Try not to get us killed," she muttered.

"He said he wasn't going to hurt us."

"And you *believe* him?"

"Seeing as how we're tied up and my gun is over there, yeah, I want to believe him."

Marissa rolled her eyes. "You're an idiot," she whispered.

"Perhaps. But I really don't think he intends to kill us. I really think he wants to confess."

"We are *fucking* tied up!" she hissed. "Do you not watch TV? This is what happens before they kill you!"

They both looked up as Monsignor Bernard returned, laboring to carry a chair. He finally set it down, sliding it closer to them. They watched in silence as he settled his bulk into the chair, facing them.

"I do not plan to kill you, Ms. Goddard. But you are right, Detective. You should be able to ask questions of me. There is no other way for you to understand what happened." He lifted the sleeve of his linen robe, dabbing at the sweat on his brow. "We shall think of it as a trial, if you like."

Casey glanced at Marissa. "Questions?"

Marissa shook her head. "Feel free, O'Connor."

"Okay." Casey met Bernard's eyes, noting the sadness, noting the hopelessness. No, he had no intention of killing them. He was already defeated. She honestly believed all he wanted to do was clear his conscience. "*Why* is much too broad of a question," she said. "Let's start with Father Michael. You didn't kill him."

"No."

"But you had Juan do it, correct?"

He nodded. "Yes. I . . . I coerced Juan into it, yes. I told him I had found cocaine in his truck. I told him I was going to call the police. Unless, of course, he carried out God's command. I told him Father Michael had sinned. And he must be punished."

"Because he was having an affair with Father Tim?"

"Yes." He smiled. "I'm surprised you found that bit of information, Detective. I thought I had it well buried."

Casey shrugged. "Well, I'm a detective. Some things can't stay buried." She cleared her throat. "But why would you kill Father Michael and not Father Tim?"

He frowned. "Why would I kill Father Tim?"

"Because he was having an affair. I mean, you wanted Father Michael killed. Why not both of them?"

Bernard shook his head. "You misunderstand, Detective. The affair was an excuse. That's all. I didn't even know about the affair until he told me."

It was Casey's turn to frown. "He who?"

"Gerald. Gerald Stevens."

"*Mayor* Stevens?"

"Yes. Something you probably don't know, but they were brothers."

Casey nodded. "Yes, we were aware of that." She let out a heavy sigh. "So, Stevens told you about the affair? Not Juan? Not Alice?"

"No. Juan rarely spoke to me. We had a disagreement a few years ago. And Alice, well, Alice simply doted on Michael."

"But, why would you want him killed?"

"I didn't, Detective."

"I don't understand."

"Stevens wanted him dead."

"His own brother? Because he was having an affair, he wanted him dead? My God."

"What are you talking about? It didn't have anything to do with his affair."

"He wasn't killed because of his affair with Father Tim?"

Monsignor Bernard shook his head. "No. Why would you think that?"

Casey closed her eyes and let her head drop. "We're talking in circles here." She looked up. "Monsignor, why don't you tell us what happened. From the beginning."

"What the hell are all these people doing here?"

"It's Sunday, Hunter. Noon."

"And?"

"Some people go to church."

"Well, goddamn. It's going to be a little hard to sneak in unobserved," she said as she peered out the car window, watching them walk by in their suits and dresses.

"Then perhaps we should go back and get a *warrant*."

"Jesus Christ, Sikes, get over the warrant already. No judge is going to give us a warrant."

"Precisely my point, Hunter."

"I just want to talk to him, that's all. He's probably in church anyway. So we'll just wait for him to come out, then follow him. That's all. Just to talk. We don't need a warrant just to talk."

"Mayor Stevens came to see me one day. He said he knew that Father Tim and his brother were lovers. And he wanted to put an end to it. He asked that I have Father Tim transferred." Bernard stood, going slowly to the window and looking out. "I knew that the mayor and Bishop Lewis were friends. I knew if he took this request to Bishop Lewis, it would be granted. So I agreed." He turned back around. "In fact, I was happy to agree. They were breaking all sorts of rules of conduct, not to mention their vows. If word had gotten out, well, it would have been devastating to the church. Another scandal we would have to weather."

"So you didn't tell Bishop Lewis?"

"Yes, of course. I transferred Father Tim, but Bishop Lewis had to approve it. After I explained what I knew, he was happy to do so."

"So that was that with the affair?"

"Yes. Michael was very upset, of course. In fact, he came to see me that night. He knew his brother was behind it. He told me some very frightening things about Stevens that night. Things I later found out to be true."

"Like what?"

"When they were young, their parents divorced. Their mother was a drug addict, I understand. But Gerald began to get into trouble, to hang with the wrong crowd."

"That happens to a lot of people when parents divorce."

"Probably not as severe as this, Detective. A neighbor boy of theirs came up missing. He was never found. Father Michael told me that Gerald killed the boy. Gerald was fifteen at the time, I believe."

"Your Mayor Stevens killed someone?" Marissa asked, her voice low. "That's what this is about?"

"He killed this boy, yes. And Michael helped him bury the body. To this day, it's never been found."

"Where?" Casey asked.

"He did not tell me that, Detective."

"Okay, so was this an accident? Or murder?"

"His throat was cut with a knife."

"Jesus," Marissa murmured. "That's why I'm here, isn't it?"

"Yes."

"Okay, wait a minute," Casey said, frustrated. "What the hell

201

are you talking about?"

"The cover-up was a cover-up, O'Connor."

"Huh?"

"I was here on the pretence of protecting the church from a sex scandal. To hide Father Michael's affair. Divert attention."

Casey shook her head. "Don't confuse me. I'm lost as it is." She flexed her arms. "And these goddamn handcuffs aren't helping."

"I'm sorry, Detective. You will be free soon enough, I imagine."

Casey took a deep breath. "Okay, why was Father Michael murdered?"

"He threatened to go to the police about the killing."

"Why? Why now after all this time?"

"Because Gerald was popular. And Gerald was running for the Senate. And because Gerald was being backed by some unscrupulous parties."

"That's it?"

"Do you know the power a U.S. Senator has, Detective?"

"Obviously not."

"Michael did not want that power to be in his hands."

"I guess I don't understand your role in all of this then."

The monsignor paced heavily across the room, his breathing labored. Casey watched him, wondering if he would tell them.

"He threatened to expose me," he finally said, his back still to them.

Casey glanced at Marissa questioningly, but she shook her head. She waited, hoping he would elaborate, but he stood still, his head bowed. She couldn't stand the silence. "Expose what, Monsignor?"

He turned his head toward them, then looked away. "Of course, exposing me would expose Bishop Lewis. I couldn't allow that to happen. I owe Bishop Lewis too much." He laughed bitterly. "Of course he knew that. He knew I would never allow Bishop Lewis's name to be dragged through the mud. I mean, I owe him my career, my life even."

Casey swallowed nervously. "Expose what?" she asked again. She saw his shoulders sag, saw his head drop to his chest.

"Years ago . . . I had a fondness for . . . for young boys," he said in barely a whisper. "A sinner I was, yes," he said, his voice rising. "A sinner." He finally turned to face them. "I did it," he said, nodding rapidly. "I did it, yes. I took them into the rectory, I took them behind the altar, I took them into the choir room." He raised his hands, his head tilted back, eyes closed. "And I enjoyed it. Yes, I did."

The room was quiet for a moment, then his hands suddenly dropped to his sides. "But someone told. Someone couldn't keep quiet." He shook his head. "Someone went to Bishop Lewis." He went back to stand by the window. He fumbled with the latch, struggling to open it, finally lifting the window a few inches, letting in cold air. Then he rested his forehead against the pane. "We were in Kansas City at the time. Bishop Lewis was being sent here." He turned around, looking at them. "I was allowed to come with him. I spent three years in therapy. I never touched another boy again," he said, his voice faltering. "I thought it was all over with, all behind me."

"How did Mayor Stevens find out?" Marissa asked.

"I don't know. But he knew. He knew it all. He knew Bishop Lewis had covered it up. He knew I'd fled Kansas City to come here. He knew it all."

"And he threatened you?" Casey asked.

"He said he would expose both of us, yes." He started pacing slowly in front of them. "It would have ruined Bishop Lewis. They would have gone back, they would have reviewed everything he'd ever done, every little thing he kept buried, and they would have found out. They would have found out everything. He said he would expose us. Unless I . . . unless I took care of Michael." He closed his eyes. "And Juan, well, he was the obvious choice because no way I could do anything myself," he added quickly. "But he had someone watching, he must have, because he knew everything." He paused. "He knew Juan was starting to talk, that Juan was about to break. So he came to me, brought me a gun," he said, pointing at the table. "He said I had to take care of Juan, because if I didn't, Juan would tell everyone that I'd ordered him to kill Father Michael." His fists clenched together. "I had to take care of Juan. And it was so easy. I knocked on the door and he let me in. And I shot him. And then I walked out. Just like that."

"How did you leave the building so fast?" Casey asked, her mind racing, trying to remember the details of the report.

"No. I went into the empty apartment across the hall. Juan was the janitor there, so he had a key. And I waited until the police came. Then I walked out and blended with the crowd. It was too easy."

Casey nodded. No wonder he hadn't had to race up and then down three flights of stairs.

"But the housekeeper?" Marissa asked. "Why her?"

"Poor Alice. She was about to talk. She knew too much."

"Knew what?" Casey asked. "Knew about Father Tim?"

"Yes, she knew. Of course she knew. She never bothered to tell me though, did she?" He paced again, his shoulders lifting with each breath he took. "But she knew Juan. She knew Juan better than anyone except maybe Michael. And she knew Juan would never kill Michael." He flicked his gaze out the window. "She looked at me and I knew she knew. I could see it in her eyes. At the funeral, she looked at me. And I knew she knew."

"So you killed her too?" Marissa asked.

His head whipped around. "I didn't want to. But he told me I had to. He said if she suspected, then she would go to the police. And the police were visiting her nearly everyday. They were trying to break her. It was just a matter of time."

Casey shook her head, remembering her visit to Alice Hagen.

"She didn't know anything. All we were trying to get out of her was the name of his lover. That's the angle our investigation was focusing on. Nothing about you, nothing about the mayor."

Marissa laughed then, a bitter laugh. "This is all just too much," she finally said. "Too much. It had absolutely nothing to do with his affair that I was trying to cover up." She was shaking her head. "Amazing. Three people are dead. All because some man wants to be a senator." She tried to raise her arms up but the rope around her waist prevented it. "And you allowed it. You're a goddamn priest, for God's sake!" she yelled. "How could you?"

Casey moved her leg, kicking her lightly against her shin. "Calm down," she hissed.

"I will not calm down!"

"Okay, the people are almost gone, so where the hell is he?"

"Maybe he's doing confession or something."

"Wait. Her. I know her," Tori said, recognizing the receptionist. She bolted out the door before Sikes could comment. She trotted down the sidewalk, trying to catch her. "Excuse me. Hang on a second."

The woman finally stopped, turning to face Tori.

"I don't know if you remember me. I'm Detective Hunter."

"Yes, of course, Detective."

"I'm looking for Monsignor Bernard. Is he still in church?"

"No. He wasn't at Mass this morning." She frowned. "Odd. I don't recall him ever not being here."

Tori nodded, rubbing the back of her neck as she tried to decide what to do. "Can you take me to his office?"

"Oh, well, I doubt he's in his office."

Tori smiled. "Just in case. It's very important."

"Okay, well, sure. I suppose I can. I've got my key to the building with me."

Tori turned and motioned for Sikes to join her. "Hang on a

second," she said, waiting until Sikes came over. "This is John Sikes, my partner."

"Oh. You had a woman partner with you last time." She held her hand out. "It's nice to meet you, Mr. Sikes," she said politely. "I'm Susan Ames."

John smiled charmingly. "Detective Sikes, ma'am."

Tori rolled her eyes, sighing heavily. "Can we go?"

"Of course." She smiled at John. "As I was just telling Detective Hunter here, I doubt seriously that Monsignor Bernard is in his office. He never misses Mass. Maybe he's ill this morning."

"Well, we just have a couple of questions. We won't take up much of his time."

"Oh? Is this about Father Michael still? Or poor Mrs. Hagen?" She tsked. "So awful what happened. Just tragedies all the way around. Makes you almost afraid to be alone in your own home. You just never know what could happen."

"Yes, it was terrible."

"And her poor husband. I hear he passed out from shock and they nearly lost him too."

Tori paused at the steps to the offices, waiting for Susan Ames to find her key to the building as she rummaged through her purse.

"Here it is," she said, holding up a set up keys. But when she reached for the door, it opened. "That's odd. It's always kept locked on Sundays. Maybe he's in his office after all."

Tori looked quickly at Sikes, then pushed the door open, leaving them in the lobby. But all was quiet and dark, no sign that anyone was about.

"His office is down that hallway, right?" she asked, already heading in that direction.

"Yes, but I can call him if you'd like," Susan offered.

"No, thanks. We'll just pop in."

Susan hurried after them. "Really, he doesn't like people to just barge in on him. I should call him first."

But Tori had already reached his office door. It was closed and locked. She raised her hand, knocking sharply. "Monsignor Bernard? Are you there?"

There was no sound from inside.

Tori stepped back, pointing at the door. "Open it up, Ms. Ames."

She pursed her lips. "Oh, no. I can't do that. He would not approve."

Tori pulled her weapon, holding it in front of her. "Open the goddamn door."

Sikes stared at Tori, his eyes wide. He finally moved between them, his back to Tori. "Please, Susan. He might be inside. He could be hurt or something. We just want to check on him."

"Well, I just . . . I don't think he's inside . . . but, but—" She looked nervously at Tori and the gun in her hand. "If you're ordering me to open his door . . ."

"I'm ordering you to open his door," Tori said calmly. "It's okay. You won't get into trouble."

"Yeah, but we might," Sikes muttered under his breath.

As soon as the lock was turned, Tori guided Susan out of the way behind them, then pushed open the door. But the office was dark.

She flipped on the lights. The room looked undisturbed. "Does he keep his desk locked?"

"Yes. Yes, he does."

Tori slid his chair out from behind his desk. "You have a key?"

"I . . . I can't get into his desk, no."

Tori stared at her. "You have a key?"

"I . . . I let you into his office. That's bad enough, Detective. I'll lose my job for sure if I unlock his desk."

Tori sighed, letting her shoulders sag, then pointed her gun at his desk. "So you'd rather I just shoot my way into it?"

"Oh, no! No, no, please," she said, moving forward. "This

desk was made in Rome. It's very old. He would just die if something happened to it."

Tori fixed her with a glare. "Then open the desk," she said quietly.

Susan glanced at Sikes, but he shook his head. "There's no reasoning with her when she gets like this, Susan. I'd go ahead and open it if I were you."

"Then let it be noted that I'm doing it against my will and at gunpoint," she said.

Tori arched an eyebrow. "Nobody's pointing a gun at you. Yet," she added. "Now, open up his desk."

She sorted through the keys on her chain. "I don't know what you hope to find here," she said. "It's just his personal things."

"My patience is wearing thin, Ms. Ames."

"Fine. Here's the key. You open it."

"Jesus Christ," Tori murmured as she ripped the key from her hand. She slipped it into the lock on the middle drawer, turning it until they heard the click of the bolt slipping back. But it wasn't the middle drawer she opened. She pulled out the top drawer on the left, staring inside at the lavender-colored tube of lotion. She picked it up, eyebrows raised, then tossed it to Sikes.

"Wow. Organic Lavender Hand Cream by Peaceful Herbs Farm. Imagine that."

"Yeah. Imagine."

"Shame we didn't have a warrant," he murmured.

"It's a special brand," Susan said. "He orders it from California."

Sikes tossed it back into the drawer. "Now what?"

Tori turned to Susan. "Where is he?"

"I told you I don't know. Like I said, if he's ill, maybe he stayed home."

"And home is?"

"He has one of the houses there, down past the rectory."

"Fine. You're going to take us."

"Oh, I really need to get going." Susan fidgeted. "I'm due at my mother's for lunch. It's a Sunday tradition."

Tori closed the drawer and locked it again, tossing the keys to Susan with a smile. "Gonna have to miss lunch, I'm afraid."

"Oh, I can't. I've never missed Sunday lunch."

"Now, you really don't want us to arrest you, do you?"

Her eyes widened. "*Arrest*? Why?"

"Oh, how about hindering a police investigation?" She shot a glance at Sikes. "Or failure to assist? That's a good one."

"But I've—"

"Come on, let's go." Tori flipped the light switch, then pulled the door closed. "Lock it up."

"What about O'Connor?" Sikes asked.

"Call her again, would you?" She took Susan's arm. "Marissa Goddard. She's got an office here."

"Yes, it's down the other hallway."

"Yes, I know. We might need your key for that one also," she said, keeping Susan beside her with a firm grip on her elbow.

"Just goes to voice mail," Sikes said as he closed his phone.

"I'm going to kill her."

"Well, you know, it's Sunday. She's allowed a day off."

"Well, we're not taking the day off, are we?"

"And technically, the case she was working on is closed," he added.

"Yeah? So I suppose she didn't *technically* drag my ass out to West Texas in the middle of blizzard for that same closed case?"

"She's got a little bit of a renegade in her, doesn't she?"

"You think?"

"No wonder you like her."

Tori stopped at Marissa's door, but there was no need to use the key. It was unlocked. She frowned, seeing the laptop and purse, her cell phone beside it. She noticed the piece of paper tucked under the phone. It was from Casey. She handed it to John.

"So she was here," he said, handing the paper back to Tori.

Tori stared at the desk, wondering what was going on. "Who would leave their phone and purse out like this? Either you take it with you or you put it in a drawer, right?" She touched the laptop. It was cold. "So O'Connor comes looking for her, finds it just like this and leaves her a note." Tori looked at Sikes. "Makes no sense."

"What? The purse being out or O'Connor's note?"

"If O'Connor left a note for her to call, why isn't her phone on?"

"Maybe they hooked up, so she just turned it off," he suggested.

Tori stared at him. "Something's not right."

CHAPTER THIRTY-ONE

Casey's and Marissa's eyes met as they watched Monsignor Bernard fall to his knees in the middle of the room, arms outstretched as he prayed, his murmured words too low for them to make out.

"Any suggestions?" Casey murmured.

"You're the cop. You figure it out."

"Well, my main problem, besides being handcuffed, is that I don't have a key for the cuffs."

"Figures."

Casey looked at the rope holding Marissa prisoner. "I'll say this, he knows how to tie knots. There must be four or five of them."

"And don't you have a knife or something tucked away?" she whispered.

"What? You think I'm MacGyver or what?"

Marissa frowned. "Who?"

"You know, TV show back in the Eighties. MacGyver."

Marissa glared at her. "You want to talk TV shows? Now? Please say someone knows you're here. Please say Hunter is coming."

Casey grinned. "I didn't think you even liked Hunter."

Marissa flailed her arms, the skin reddening where the ropes cut into them. She finally stopped and shook her head. "Did I really sleep with you?"

"Don't you remember?" Casey wiggled her eyebrows. "You begged me to stay, if I remember correctly."

"I must have been out of my mind."

"No doubt." Casey motioned to Bernard. "How long should we let him do that?"

"He's praying. Trying to cleanse his soul."

"Yeah? Well, we don't have that long." She cleared her throat. "Monsignor?" She waited, but he didn't move, his voice still low and mumbled. "Monsignor Bernard?"

His arms lowered, but his lips continued to move in prayer. Finally, he turned, his eyes clearly dazed, damp with tears.

"Excuse me, but shouldn't we do something?" Casey asked. "I mean, call the police, go after the mayor, something."

He struggled to get to his feet, grabbing onto the edge of the desk to pull himself up. He tugged at the sleeves of his robe, straightening them, then went to the window, opening it farther as beads of sweat dotted his brow. He leaned on the windowsill, his gaze far away as he looked out over the church grounds.

"Go after the mayor?" He shook his head. "And do what?"

"Well, you've got to give a statement. Granted, it'll be your word against his, since—"

"Since everyone else is dead?" He took a deep breath, lifting his sleeve to again wipe at his brow. "Weren't you listening, Detective? I won't have Bishop Lewis exposed. I won't have my past exposed. It ends here."

"But without your testimony, there's no way we'd have any evidence against him."

"Even with my testimony, Detective, Mayor Stevens is untouchable."

"Nobody is untouchable."

He smiled sadly. "Tell her, Ms. Goddard. Tell her how it all works. Tell her about cover-ups and political maneuvers. Tell her how easily the media is manipulated. Tell her how the police chief is but a puppet of Mayor Stevens. Then tell her why no charges will ever be brought against Mayor Stevens." He looked out the window again. "Tell her he is untouchable."

Tori walked out into the sunshine, the air remarkably colder than the heat of the building. Looking around, she turned again to Susan Ames. Where is his house?"

"It's . . . it's just down the street here. But maybe we should just call him."

"Maybe you should just show us where it is."

Tori started walking, pulling Susan along beside her.

Casey watched as Monsignor Bernard carefully removed the cross from around his neck, placing it gently on the purple cloth on the table.

"Tainted," he murmured.

Then he removed the stole, methodically folding it before placing it beside the cross. Unbuttoning the white robe, he struggled to pull his arms through the sleeves. This, he simply wadded it up and tossed unceremoniously on a chair before turning to face them.

"I am obviously unfit to wear the garments of Christ." He looked down and she actually felt sorry for him as he struggled to catch his breath. "Please know that in my heart—in my soul—

I deeply regret what I have done." He lifted his head. "It is over now. It is in Christ's hands."

Suddenly he turned, taking giant, lumbering steps to the window and then flung himself out, the glass shattering as his bulk slammed against it.

Seconds passed before screaming drifted up from below, the sounds weaving their way into the room.

"Holy shit," Casey said. "Holy *fucking* shit." She tried to stand, then fell back into the chair. "Goddamn cuffs," she murmured. "Are you okay?"

Marissa stared, her eyes wide. "I can't . . . I can't believe it. I just can't believe it."

"And I can't believe we're goddamn tied to these fucking chairs!" she yelled as she twisted her wrists against the cuffs. She turned to Marissa. "Got any ideas?"

Susan Ames screamed, the sound echoing through the courtyard, her voice rising as each second passed.

"What the fuck?"

"Oh, my God."

Tori ran to the man, stopping short at the sight of Monsignor Bernard's body impaled by the wrought iron spears that surrounded the statue of the Virgin Mary. Blood now stained the pristine effigy as it dripped slowly downward.

"Son of a bitch," she murmured.

More screams were heard as people began to gather, and Tori stepped back, looking up to the third-floor window.

"Sikes, call it in," Tori said, her eyes never leaving the third floor. "I'm going up."

"Okay, I'm going to scoot the chair around, try to get behind you so I can work on those knots."

"Why don't you have a key to your handcuffs?"

"Because I just don't."

"You've never used them before, have you?"

Casey grinned. "Well, not in the line of duty, no."

Marissa leaned her head back, eyes closed. "Tell me again why we slept together?"

Casey bounced lightly on her chair, trying to move it, coming dangerously close to tipping over. "Because you couldn't keep your hands off me, that's why. And who could blame you? I'm a good catch."

Marissa's retort died as the door slammed open. Tori stood there, her weapon drawn.

"About goddamn time, Hunter. I was about to perform miracles here."

Tori laughed as she holstered her weapon. "I swear, O'Connor, I see you'll do just about anything to be alone with this woman."

"Yeah, right. She seems to have lost her bedside manner, being tied up."

"Is that right, Ms. Goddard?"

"Let me just say I never thought I'd be happy to see you, Hunter."

"Hunter, you're not going to believe what just happened," Casey said, watching as Tori knelt behind Marissa's chair. "Yeah, untie her first. She's getting cranky." She looked back at Tori. "Anyway, he jumped right through that window like he thought he could fly or something."

"Yeah, well, trust me, he couldn't."

"Is he . . . is he dead?" Marissa asked.

"Oh, yeah. He's dead." She fumbled with the last knot, then turned to Casey. "How in the hell did you allow yourself to get cuffed?"

Casey glanced to the table. "Well, my weapon is over there."

"I see. Why is that?"

"He took it from me."

"How so?"

"He, well, he had a gun held to her head," she said, motioning to Marissa, who stood silently by rubbing her wrists.

"So you missed that day at the academy where you learn never to give up your weapon, huh?"

"Are you going to lecture me or are you going to get me out of these cuffs?"

"Got a key?"

"She doesn't have a key," Marissa said. "I assume the last time she used them for *playtime*, some woman took the key."

"O'Connor, God, you've got to get a life," Tori said as she pulled out her key ring, searching for her own handcuff key.

"We've got to talk before they get here."

"They who?"

"They . . . they," Casey said, rubbing her wrists when Tori finally freed her. "We've been tied up for hours, it seems like."

"They who, O'Connor?"

"The mayor, the chief, whoever. You know, *they*."

"What are you talking about?"

"He implicated the mayor in all this."

"What the hell are you talking about, O'Connor?"

Casey took Tori's arm and pulled her aside, away from Marissa. "The murders had nothing to do with his affair, nothing to do with trying to keep it quiet." She motioned to Marissa. "She was here to make everyone *think* it had to do with the affair. Stevens was really concerned with covering up his past."

"I don't really see the point in trying to whisper, O'Connor," Marissa said as she approached them. "I was here, you know. I heard everything." She turned to Tori. "Gerald Stevens killed a boy when he was a teen. His brother, Michael, helped bury the body. Michael threatened to tell if Stevens ran for the Senate. Seems there's some bad blood there."

Tori paced the room. "What the hell? Stevens killed someone?" She shook her head. "Unbelievable. So what was Bernard's role in all this? We know he killed Alice Hagen. They found a lotion smudge. It matched what we found in his desk. What the hell is his role in this?"

"Bernard had skeletons in his closet too. Stevens knew them. He blackmailed Bernard. Bernard blackmailed Juan. Then Stevens panicked and had Bernard kill Juan and Alice, thinking they were going to talk."

Tori shook her head again "This is crazy. Just because he said some things up here doesn't mean it's true. You can't implicate Mayor Stevens."

"You should have heard everything he told us, Hunter. It was true," Casey said.

Tori turned to Marissa. "What do you think? You knew him better than anybody."

Marissa nodded. "Yes, he was telling the truth. He couldn't live with what he did, he couldn't live if his past was exposed, and he couldn't *die* not telling someone about Mayor Stevens."

Tori stared at them. "Then when you give your statements, you better both be on the same page."

Marissa shook her head. "No way. I'm not giving a statement."

"You have to," Casey said. "It's standard procedure."

"If we tell everything that Bernard just told us, then we're next on the hit list."

"Oh, come on, this isn't some gangster movie," Casey said. "There's not going to be a hit list."

"Tell that to Alice Hagen. Or Juan Hidalgo."

"She's right," Tori said.

"Come on, Hunter. What? Are we just going to contribute to the cover-up? We're going to pretend we *don't* know what really happened?"

"No. But if what you say is true, then I'll be surprised if you're even asked to give a statement. And when *they* come, then if I were you," Tori said, looking at Marissa, too. "I'd lie my ass off and say he didn't give up a thing."

Casey looked at Marissa. "But what are we accomplishing? Four people are dead now. For what? He's still the mayor. He can still run for the Senate." She shrugged. "He's won."

"And what will we accomplish if we give our statements? Where will it go? It'll be buried, O'Connor. Buried. And then we're expendable." Marissa shook her head. "I'm not giving a statement."

Casey grasped Tori's arm. "Hunter, come on. We can't just let this go. If this was you, if you'd been the one tied up here, if you'd heard all this shit, no way you'd let this go."

"Maybe so. But right now, right here," Tori said, "I have to agree with Marissa. It'll just be buried, O'Connor. You can't win this one."

Furious, Casey spun around facing the broken window, her fists clenched. "Goddamn son of a bitch," she yelled.

CHAPTER THIRTY-TWO

The airport was crowded for a Sunday night. Casey and Marissa stopped, looking at the long line to check in luggage. Marissa set her bags down, her eyes still troubled as she looked at Casey.

Casey nodded, shoving both hands into the pockets of her jeans. "Well, we solved two murders today, got everything wrapped up all nice and tidy," she said. "Two people killed because the monsignor wanted to cover up a love affair."

"Appears that way."

"You handled the little impromptu press conference very well. The mayor seemed especially grateful. Sunday's a slow news day and all."

"Look, O'Connor, I don't like it anymore than you do." Her voice lowered. "We could have been killed today. And for what? Because some jacked-up politician is on a power trip and needed to cover up his past?" She shook her head. "I'm not proud of what I did, but it's my job. And because I'm good at my job, the mayor thinks Bernard jumped without mentioning his name even once."

"And so the mayor gets to go on his merry way while four innocent people are dead."

"Life's not fair. Life sucks," Marissa said. "Use any line you want—they're all true." She glanced at her watch. "I should get going, O'Connor."

Casey nodded. "Yeah. Sorry you missed your flight though."

Marissa shrugged. "They've got me on standby. I'm sure I'll catch the next one."

Casey shifted nervously, finally pulling her hands from her pockets. "Well, it was nice to meet you, Ms. Goddard," she said with a smile. "I quite enjoyed *most* of our time together."

Marissa laughed. "Sorry I called you an idiot." She squeezed Casey's arm. "I enjoyed meeting you too, O'Connor. And if you're ever in Boston . . ."

"Boston? Where's that?"

"Funny." Marissa reached for her bag again. "Take care of yourself, O'Connor."

Casey surprised herself both by leaning forward and placing a quick kiss on her lips. "Have a safe flight."

She turned and left without looking back. She doubted she'd ever see Marissa Goddard again. But back outside, the cold wind hit and she pulled her jacket collar up around her neck. Glancing around, she saw a familiar figure standing under a light pillar. Tori.

"What the hell are you doing here, Hunter?"

Tori pushed off the metal beam, falling into step beside Casey. "Thought you might need a friend."

"Friend? I thought you said you didn't have any friends."

Tori shrugged. "Yes. That's true. But Sam said I need to find someone besides Sikes to hang around with."

Casey laughed. "I see her point. Sikes is a little girlie—for a straight guy."

Tori bumped her shoulder lightly. "So? You okay?"

"Yeah. Why wouldn't I be?" Casey laughed sarcastically. "I'm a cop and I'm covering up a handful of murders. It's peachy."

Tori smiled. "I meant about Marissa."

"Marissa? Oh, you mean because she left?"

"Yeah."

"Oh. Well, yeah. I mean, I never did decide if I even liked her or not." She bumped Tori's shoulder playfully. "Besides, I'm kinda looking for something like you and Sam have. She wasn't it."

Tori nodded. "You'll find it."

"Maybe." They walked on in silence for a moment, then Casey sighed. "So, what are we going to do about Mayor Stevens?"

"Well, you know, I've been thinking. Maybe we should just let the media do it for us."

"What'd you mean?"

"Melissa Carter. Channel Five." Tori grinned. "She's been begging for a story. How about I give her the brother angle and see what she can dig up?"

"Like the murder of a young boy years ago?"

"Exactly."

CHAPTER THIRTY-THREE

Casey rolled over, searching for her phone. She looked at the clock, wondering who would call at this hour on a Sunday night.

"O'Connor," she answered sleepily, sitting up.

"It's me."

"Hunter? Damn, I was just in the middle of a delicious dream. This better be good."

"I'm at a crime scene. I thought you might want to come over."

Casey stood, already reaching for her jeans. "What's up?"

"Gerald Stevens is dead."

Casey nearly dropped the phone. "I'll be right there."

Casey shoved through the crowd of reporters and neighbors, dipping under the crime-scene tape after showing her badge to one of the uniformed officers. The house glowed from the outside; every light was turned on inside. The entry foyer was massive and she stood, looking for Tori in the crowded den off to the side.

Tori turned as if sensing her presence, meeting her gaze. She motioned for her to come over and Casey edged along the wall, trying to stay out of everyone's way.

"O'Connor. This is Mac Sterner. He heads up the crime unit."

Casey held out her hand. "Yes, we've met once before. Whispers outside say it was a suicide. Is that true?"

Mac shook his head. "I think it was made to appear that way. The angle's all wrong. As I was telling Hunter here, Stevens was right-handed. If you're going to shoot yourself in the head, do you use your left hand? Besides, there's no imprint from the barrel on his scalp. My guess is the gun was at least a foot or two away when it was fired." He motioned to the body. "We'll check for GSR on his hand, but my guess is we won't find any."

Casey looked at the body, her gaze lingering on what was left of his face. Nearly half his head was blown away. She raised her eyes, watching Tori.

"Give me something to go on, Mac. Where's the wife?"

"She's wasn't here, Hunter. Sikes is tracking her down," he explained.

"Any possibility she did it?"

Mac stepped back, surveying the scene. "He's standing, not sitting. He's what? Six foot three?" He walked around the body. "I'm going to just guess on the angle until we can get him cleaned up, but I'd say your shooter was about five-seven, five-eight, tops." He held his hands out in a shooting position. "I'd also guess your shooter was left-handed."

"How so?" Casey asked.

Mac held his finger to Casey's head. "The bullet wound entered from this side, at this angle. If I'm right-handed"—he

223

turned, changing hands—"it enters like this."

"Did we find the casing?"

"No. I'm sure the shooter took it with him."

"Nothing was disturbed?" Casey asked. "No break-in?"

"No. Nothing looks out of place." Tori shook her head. "We can assume Stevens knew his killer." She raised an eyebrow. "Sound familiar?"

"Yeah, sounds familiar," Casey murmured. She moved away, into the crowd, watching absently as Tori pulled her phone off her hip and answered it. "Jesus . . . Jesus Christ," she said with a slow shake of her head. She took a deep breath, then pulled out her own phone, slipping away. She dialed quickly and was surprised when Marissa answered on the first ring. "It's . . . it's me."

"Detective O'Connor, I didn't think I'd hear from you so soon."

"Yeah, well, I was just checking on you. You catch your flight okay?"

"Actually, no. It looked like it was going to be a long wait, so I decided to rent a car."

"You're going to drive all the way to Boston?"

She heard Marissa sigh, heard the subtle clearing of her throat, and she waited.

"I decided there wasn't really anything in Boston, you know. So I decided to go home. I'm heading west."

"I see." Casey went down a quiet hallway, letting the voices from the crime scene fade into the background. "Well, I wanted to pass on the latest." She paused. "Gerald Stevens is dead. Shot to death."

There was nothing but silence on the other end of the phone.

Casey tilted her head back, staring at the ceiling. "Did you hear me?"

"Yes, O'Connor. I heard. Should I say I'm sorry?"

"Why? Are you?"

"No. Are you?"

Casey shook her head. "No." She cleared her throat. "There doesn't appear to be much evidence. Hunter's got the case."

"The way I hear it, Hunter never rests until a case is solved. I'm sure she'll find the killer."

Casey sighed. "We'll see. I'm not sure her heart's really in this one."

CHAPTER THIRTY-FOUR

After a cool start, the day had warmed up nicely. Both Tori and Casey stood in short sleeves, tossing their lines into the lake.

"Great day for fishing," Casey said, glad to be out and about in the middle of the week. "Nice of Lieutenant Malone to let you have the day off."

Tori laughed. "Yeah. And nice of you to finagle one yourself. You keep hanging around, they're going to think you want to get transferred to Homicide."

"Are you kidding? You think people are just *dying* to work Homicide?"

"Funny, O'Connor."

"Yeah. Funny." She reeled her line in, then tossed it out again. "Shame about the mayor, isn't it," she said quietly.

"Yeah. Shame."

"But I guess you're glad CIU is taking over the investigation, huh?"

"For sure." Tori bent over and reached into the cooler beside her. "Want another beer?"

"Yeah." Casey leaned her rod and reel against the edge, then took the cold bottle and sat down on the deck chair Tori had pulled out. "So CIU is just going to come in and do their own thing, right?"

"Yeah."

"They don't even use your notes or anything?"

Tori opened her own beer and took a swallow. "Not like we had a lot, O'Connor. But no, they start their investigation from scratch. They'll make it look like we were incompetent and not capable of handling such a high-profile case such as this." She shrugged. "Could be true."

"Any idea what angle they'll take?"

"Rumor has it that Stevens was mixed up in drug trafficking. I mean, you saw his house. He had money from somewhere."

"Thought his wife was a socialite."

"Don't know."

"And don't care?"

"Pretty much."

They were both quiet, Tori still leaning over the side, casually watching her line float along the surface. Casey stretched her legs out, turning her face into the warm sun.

Tori tilted her head, glancing at Casey. "Marissa is left-handed, isn't she?"

Casey rolled her head lazily to the side, watching Tori. "Yeah, I believe she is."

Tori nodded, then looked back over the water. "Shame about the mayor," she said again.

Casey smiled. "So, you ever catch anything here docked at the pier?"

"No. Never."

Sam stood on the pier, shielding her eyes from the sun, watching as Tori laughed at something the other woman said. Casey O'Connor, she guessed. Smiling, she walked the few feet to the boat, pausing before going aboard.

"Hi there," she called. "May I board?"

Tori whipped around, her eyes wide. She dropped her line, nearly running across the deck. "What the hell?"

"What kind of greeting is that?"

"Sam, my God, why didn't you let me know?" Tori murmured as she pulled her close. "I can't believe you're here."

Sam closed her eyes, letting her body reacquaint itself with Tori's, letting her hands roam freely across Tori's back. "Beautiful sunny day. I took a chance you'd be out here."

Tori laughed. "You called Malone, didn't you?"

"I did." She pulled away slightly, looking into Tori's eyes. "God, I missed you," she whispered, finding Tori's mouth. She pulled away again, breathless. "I missed you so much, Tori." She slid her hand up Tori's waist, squeezing lightly at her side.

"I can't even begin to tell you, Sam. It's just so damn empty without you, you know."

"Yes, I know." She stepped back. "Now, are you going to introduce me or what?"

"Damn." Tori turned around. "Forgot you were here, O'Connor."

"Thanks a lot." Casey came over, hand outstretched. "Casey O'Connor. And since you had a lip-lock on the old girl here, I'll assume you're Sam. Nice to meet you."

Sam laughed. "Samantha Kennedy, yes. Nice to meet you, Casey."

Casey elbowed Tori playfully. "You dog. She's even prettier than her pictures."

Tori blushed and bumped Casey's shoulder in turn. "Try to

228

behave, O'Connor."

"Not possible." But she grinned. "I'll get out of your hair, though. I know you two want some time together."

Sam held up her hand. "No, no, please stay."

"No, I should go."

"Really, please stay. I've had a long flight. I just want to relax and sit in the sun for a while." Sam looked at Tori and smiled. "You don't mind, do you?"

"No, no. I haven't seen you in what feels like months. What are a few more hours?"

"Great. Then I'll have a beer with you guys." Sam hooked her arm with Casey's, leading her back into the sunshine. "And I'm dying to meet the person Tori Hunter has let into her life," she said in a low whisper. "It doesn't happen often," she added.

"She's just a big old teddy bear," Casey said with a laugh. "Of course, I think she takes offense at my use of the *old* word."

Tori watched them, feeling an odd sense of familiarity at the sight of them laughing together. She walked over, handing each of them a beer. "Are you telling stories about me already, O'Connor?"

"Oh, lighten up. As if we're talking about you. Not *everybody* talks about you, Hunter."

Curious, Tori let her glance slide to Sam. "So? What are you doing back?"

"The mayor, what else? I didn't have a chance to call you. They had us packed and on a plane as soon as we got back from the field. I guess you know by now CIU's taking over the investigation."

Tori nodded. "Yeah. That's how I got a day off."

"They want Travis to head it up."

Tori looked briefly at Casey. "So does that mean you'll be on the team too?"

229

Sam nodded. "Yeah. I get pulled from Homicide in the middle of our case only to be assigned back on the team. How weird is that?"

"Yeah. Ironic," Casey said. "And I guess you heard all about the monsignor and all."

"Just briefly from Tori. I haven't had a chance to read the file or anything."

Tori leaned over the edge of the boat. "You going to tell her about Marissa or what?"

"What do you mean?" she asked, hesitation in her voice.

Tori smiled, glancing back at her. "You know, your little afternoon get-together there at the hotel."

Casey ducked her head. "Do we have to?"

Sam laughed. "You slept with her?"

Casey shrugged. "I liked her. I mean, I know everyone thought she was a hard-ass and didn't care about the case, but I think deep down, she really cared."

Tori and Casey exchanged glances, both nodding.

"Yeah, she did care," Casey said again. "She cared a lot."

Casey looked at Tori, their eyes holding. She raised an eyebrow questioningly and Tori knew what she was asking. With just a slight shake of her head, Tori hoped she conveyed all Casey needed to know.

It was one secret Tori would keep from Sam.

Publications from
BELLA BOOKS, INC.
The best in contemporary lesbian fiction

P.O. Box 10543, Tallahassee, FL 32302
Phone: 800-729-4992
www.bellabooks.com

ASPEN'S EMBERS by Diane Tremain Braund. Will Aspen choose the woman she loves . . . or the forest she hopes to preserve . . .   978-1-59493-102-4 $14.95

THE COTTAGE by Gerri Hill. *The Cottage* is the heartbreaking story of two women who meet by chance . . . or did they? A love so destined it couldn't be denied . . . stolen moments to be cherished forever.   978-1-59493-096-6 $13.95

FANTASY: Untrue Stories of Lesbian Passion edited by Barbara Johnson and Therese Szymanski. Lie back and let Bella's bad girls take you on an erotic journey through the greatest bedtime stories never told.   978-1-59493-101-7 $15.95

SISTERS' FLIGHT by Jeanne G'Fellers. *SISTER'S FLIGHT* is the highly anticipated sequel to *NO SISTER OF MINE* and *SISTER LOST SISTER FOUND*.   978-1-59493-116-1 $13.95

BRAGGIN RIGHTS by Kenna White. Taylor Fleming is a thirty-six year-old Texas rancher who covets her independence. She finds her cowgirl independence tested by neighboring rancher Jen Holland.   978-1-59493-095-9 $13.95

BRILLIANT by Ann Roberts. Respected sociology professor, Diane Cole finds her views on love challenged by her own heart, as she fights the attraction she feels for a woman half her age.   978-1-59493-115-4 $13.95

THE EDUCATION OF ELLIE by Jackie Calhoun. When Ellie sees her childhood friend for the first time in thirty years she is tempted to resume their long lost friendship. But with the years come a lot of baggage and the two women struggle with who they are now while fighting the painful memories of their first parting. Will they be able to move past their history to start again?   978-1-59493-092-8 $13.95

DATE NIGHT CLUB by Saxon Bennett. *Date Night Club* is a dark romantic comedy about the pitfalls of dating in your thirties . . .   978-1-59493-094-2 $13.95

PLEASE FORGIVE ME by Megan Carter. Laurel Becker is on the verge of losing the two most important things in her life—her current lover, Elaine Alexander, and the Lavender Page bookstore. Will Elaine and Laurel manage to work through their misunderstandings and rebuild their life together?   978-1-59493-091-1 $13.95

WHISKEY AND OAK LEAVES by Jaime Clevenger. Meg meets June, a single woman running a horse ranch in the California Sierra foothills. The two become quick friends and it isn't long before Meg is looking for more than just a friendship. But June has no interest in developing a deeper relationship with Meg. She is, after all, not the least bit interested in women . . . or is she? Neither of these two women is prepared for what lies ahead . . .   978-1-59493-093-5 $13.95

SUMTER POINT by KG MacGregor. As Audie surrenders her heart to Beth, she begins to distance herself from the reckless habits of her youth. Just as they're ready to meet in the middle, their future is thrown into doubt by a duty Beth can't ignore. It all comes to a head on the river at Sumter Point.   978-1-59493-089-8 $13.95

THE TARGET by Gerri Hill. Sara Michaels is the daughter of a prominent senator who has been receiving death threats against his family. In an effort to protect Sara, the FBI recruits homicide detective Jaime Hutchinson to secretly provide the protection they are so certain Sara will need. Will Sara finally figure out who is behind the death threats? And will Jaime realize the truth—and be able to save Sara before it's too late?
978-1-59493-082-9 $13.95

REALITY BYTES by Jane Frances. In this sequel to *Reunion*, follow the lives of four friends in a romantic tale that spans the globe and proves that you can cross the whole of cyberspace only to find love a few suburbs away . . .   978-1-59493-079-9 $13.95

MURDER CAME SECOND by Jessica Thomas. Broadway's bad-boy genius, Paul Carlucci, has chosen *Hamlet* for his latest production. To the delight of some and despair of others, he has selected Provincetown's amphitheatre for his opening gala. But suddenly Alex Peres realizes that the wrong people are falling down. And the moaning is all to realistic. Someone must not be shooting blanks . . .
978-1-59493-081-2 $13.95

SKIN DEEP by Kenna White. Jordan Griffin has been given a new assignment: Track down and interview one-time nationally renowned broadcast journalist Reece McAllister. Much to her surprise, Jordan comes away with far more than just a story . . .
978-1-59493-78-2 $13.95

FINDERS KEEPERS by Karin Kallmaker. *Finders Keepers*, the quest for the perfect mate in the 21st century, joins Karin Kallmaker's *Just Like That* and her other incomparable novels about lesbian love, lust and laughter.   1-59493-072-4 $13.95

OUT OF THE FIRE by Beth Moore. Author Ann Covington feels at the top of the world when told her book is being made into a movie. Then in walks Casey Duncan the actress who is playing the lead in her movie. Will Casey turn Ann's world upside down?
1-59493-088-0 $13.95

STAKE THROUGH THE HEART: NEW EXPLOITS OF TWILIGHT LESBIANS by Karin Kallmaker, Julia Watts, Barbara Johnson and Therese Szymanski. The playful quartet that penned the acclaimed *Once Upon A Dyke* are dimming the lights for journeys into worlds of breathless seduction.   1-59493-071-6 $15.95

THE HOUSE ON SANDSTONE by KG MacGregor. Carly Griffin returns home to Leland and finds that her old high school friend Justine is awakening more than just old memories.   1-59493-076-7 $13.95

WILD NIGHTS: MOSTLY TRUE STORIES OF WOMEN LOVING WOMEN edited by Therese Szymanski. 264 pp. 23 new stories from today's hottest erotic writers are sure to give you your wildest night ever! 1-59493-069-4 $15.95

COYOTE SKY by Gerri Hill. 248 pp. Sheriff Lee Foxx is trying to cope with the realization that she has fallen in love for the first time. And fallen for author Kate Winters, who is technically unavailable. Will Lee fight to keep Kate in Coyote? 1-59493-065-1 $13.95

VOICES OF THE HEART by Frankie J. Jones. 264 pp. A series of events force Erin to swear off love as she tries to break away from the woman of her dreams. Will Erin ever find the key to her future happiness? 1-59493-068-6 $13.95

SHELTER FROM THE STORM by Peggy J. Herring. 296 pp. A story about family and getting reacquainted with one's past that shows that sometimes you don't appreciate what you have until you almost lose it. 1-59493-064-3 $13.95

WRITING MY LOVE by Claire McNab. 192 pp. Romance writer Vonny Smith believes she will be able to woo her editor Diana through her writing. 1-59493-063-5 $13.95

PAID IN FULL by Ann Roberts. 200 pp. Ari Adams will need to choose between the debts of the past and the promise of a happy future. 1-59493-059-7 $13.95

ROMANCING THE ZONE by Kenna White. 272 pp. Liz's world begins to crumble when a secret from her past returns to Ashton. 1-59493-060-0 $13.95

SIGN ON THE LINE by Jaime Clevenger. 204 pp. Alexis Getty, a flirtatious delivery driver is committed to finding the rightful owner of a mysterious package. 1-59493-052-X $13.95

END OF WATCH by Clare Baxter. 256 pp. LAPD Lieutenant L.A. Franco Frank follows the lone clue down the unlit steps of memory to a final, unthinkable resolution. 1-59493-064-4 $13.95

BEHIND THE PINE CURTAIN by Gerri Hill. 280 pp. Jacqueline returns home after her father's death and comes face-to-face with her first crush. 1-59493-057-0 $13.95

18TH & CASTRO by Karin Kallmaker. 200 pp. First-time couplings and couples who know how to mix lust and love make 18th & Castro the hottest address in the city by the bay. 1-59493-066-X $13.95

JUST THIS ONCE by KG MacGregor. 200 pp. Mindful of the obligations back home that she must honor, Wynne Connelly struggles to resist the fascination and allure that a particular woman she meets on her business trip represents. 1-59493-087-2 $13.95

ANTICIPATION by Terri Breneman. 240 pp. Two women struggle to remain professional as they work together to find a serial killer. 1-59493-055-4 $13.95

OBSESSION by Jackie Calhoun. 240 pp. Lindsey's life is turned upside down when Sarah comes into the family nursery in search of perennials. 1-59493-058-9 $13.95

BENEATH THE WILLOW by Kenna White. 240 pp. A torch that still burns brightly even after twenty-five years threatens to consume two childhood friends. 1-59493-053-8 $13.95

SISTER LOST, SISTER FOUND by Jeanne G'Fellers. 224 pp. The highly anticipated sequel to *No Sister of Mine*. 1-59493-056-2 $13.95

THE WEEKEND VISITOR by Jessica Thomas. 240 pp. In this latest Alex Peres mystery, Alex is asked to investigate an assault on a local woman but finds that her client may have more secrets than she lets on. 1-59493-054-6 $13.95

THE KILLING ROOM by Gerri Hill. 392 pp. How can two women forget and go their separate ways? 1-59493-050-3 $12.95

PASSIONATE KISSES by Megan Carter. 240 pp. Will two old friends run from love? 1-59493-051-1 $12.95

ALWAYS AND FOREVER by Lyn Denison. 224 pp. The girl next door turns Shannon's world upside down. 1-59493-049-X $12.95

BACK TALK by Saxon Bennett. 200 pp. Can a talk show host find love after heartbreak? 1-59493-028-7 $12.95

THE PERFECT VALENTINE: EROTIC LESBIAN VALENTINE STORIES edited by Barbara Johnson and Therese Szymanski—from Bella After Dark. 328 pp. Stories from the hottest writers around. 1-59493-061-9 $14.95

MURDER AT RANDOM by Claire McNab. 200 pp. The Sixth Denise Cleever Thriller. Denise realizes the fate of thousands is in her hands. 1-59493-047-3 $12.95

THE TIDES OF PASSION by Diana Tremain Braund. 240 pp. Will Susan be able to hold it all together and find the one woman who touches her soul? 1-59493-048-1 $12.95

JUST LIKE THAT by Karin Kallmaker. 240 pp. Disliking each other—and everything they stand for—even before they meet, Toni and Syrah find feelings can change, just like that. 1-59493-025-2 $12.95

WHEN FIRST WE PRACTICE by Therese Szymanski. 200 pp. Brett and Allie are once again caught in the middle of murder and intrigue. 1-59493-045-7 $12.95

REUNION by Jane Frances. 240 pp. Cathy Braithwaite seems to have it all: good looks, money and a thriving accounting practice . . . 1-59493-046-5 $12.95

BELL, BOOK & DYKE: NEW EXPLOITS OF MAGICAL LESBIANS by Kallmaker, Watts, Johnson and Szymanski. 360 pp. Reluctant witches, tempting spells and skyclad beauties—delve into the mysteries of love, lust and power in this quartet of novellas. 1-59493-023-6 $14.95

ARTIST'S DREAM by Gerri Hill. 320 pp. When Cassie meets Luke Winston, she can no longer deny her attraction to women . . . 1-59493-042-2 $12.95

NO EVIDENCE by Nancy Sanra. 240 pp. Private investigator Tally McGinnis once again returns to the horror-filled world of a serial killer. 1-59493-043-04 $12.95

WHEN LOVE FINDS A HOME by Megan Carter. 280 pp. What will it take for Anna and Rona to find their way back to each other again? 1-59493-041-4 $12.95

MEMORIES TO DIE FOR by Adrian Gold. 240 pp. Rachel attempts to avoid her attraction to the charms of Anna Sigurdson . . . 1-59493-038-4 $12.95

SILENT HEART by Claire McNab. 280 pp. Exotic lesbian romance. 1-59493-044-9 $12.95